AWAKE

Also by Andrew Palmer

Whirlwind: Based on a True Story

Dark Frontier

Dark Frontier: The Awakening

ANDREW PALMER

SYNAPZ PRODUCTIONS
TORONTO
WWW.SYNAPZPRODUCTIONS.COM

This is a work of fiction. All of the characters, organizations, and events portrayed in this novel are either products of the author's imagination or are used fictitiously.

AWAKE. Copyright © 2020 by Synapz Productions. All rights reserved. Published in Toronto, Canada. No part of this book may be used or reproduced in any manner whatsoever without written permission except in the case of brief quotations embodied in critical articles or reviews. For information, contact Synapz Productions www.synapzproductions.com

Book Design by Andrew Palmer.
Astonished font by Misprinted Type.

ISBN-13: 979-8-684-24593-0

This book is dedicated to COVID-19
For making me stay home to write it

We're born alone, we live alone, we die alone.
Only through our love and friendship can we create
the illusion for the moment that we're not alone.

-Orson Welles

CHAPTER 1 – DAYDREAMING

And then it was dark.

The ionic ripples jolted through his body with a cascade of euphoric bliss. Intentional fireworks deployed in a test-signal pattern by the hypoxia-induced state of self-preservation. His mind, utterly desperate to maintain control of its body, felt as though it had discovered the portal to another dimension; and in a sense this was true, for Eddie Morrison was drowning.

Surrounded by darkness precipitating into a cold turbulent blue, the light rays were scattered through ocean water and focused beyond his adolescent retina, creating a nightmarish blurred reality. It was enough to notice his arms wildly thrashing about as they grew numb and desperate.

Then suddenly, a new symphonic movement exploded at high tempo. Sound waves of vibrating air molecules jostled past escaping fluid to bang a distress signal on his tiny eardrums. Eddie's head bobbed in and out of the water between gasps of salty choked confusion.

None of the horror compared, however, to the excruciating terror that had wrapped itself around his leg. A thousand microscopic barbed daggers of venomous rage sent sharp reminders coursing through his paralyzed body that it was not yet dead.

He froze in muted agony and sank below the surface, looking downward at the unwitting monster that threatened his existence. Bubbles of fear danced violently from his mouth, until a spasm inhaled sheer panic and was quickly stifled by a loss of will in the consuming void.

Or was it the sound?

Something reminded him about the sound; that droning innocuous warning that the garbage chute was re-aligning. It was almost like screaming under water…

Nope. It was definitely the garbage chute.

"Damnit." Edward snapped back to reality as the LED indicated its default setting. He reached out to press the organics button, and an incessant tone underscored metallic reverberations from several stories below.

"Daydreaming, again?"

The voice reminded him of someone else and Edward wondered if his mind intentionally played tricks, or was it just delayed realization – like when you buy a white car and suddenly notice all the other white cars out there?

Edward glanced over his shoulder to find Cura smiling at him. She was an empathetic and friendly neighbor from down the hall, who always had a way of making Edward feel uncomfortable.

"Oh hey, Cura. No, it's just this new system. I always forget."

The machine chimed and Edward spun back with relief to stuff his garbage bag into the mouth of the chute. He could sense Cura's eyes studying him, trying to wake up whatever inner light she imagined was buried deep inside his subconscious.

Why wouldn't she just leave him alone?

He turned back and forced a smile, "Sorry about that! I'm sure you probably have a client waiting for you."

Cura blocked the entrance of the garbage room and Edward anxiously contemplated the best way to get past her without appearing rude.

Her smile was warm and sincere, "As much as I'd love to, I'm not qualified to see patients in my home office yet. But you're welcome to come by any time."

Edward had seen it a million times before, on a million different people, and knew all too well that façade of teeth and lips concealed darker truths more often than not.

"Thanks, but—"

"Pro bono, of course," she interrupted, "We could discuss that recurring dream you keep having. Is that what you were just thinking about?"

Edward shook his head, "That wasn't a dream. I was just…" He struggled to recall the moments prior to Cura arriving and considered the possibility he really was daydreaming.

"No pressure," she insisted, "Just thought I'd put it out there! I would really love to help, but truthfully, the hours also count towards my psychiatry license."

And there it was.

He almost sneered, "Oh, well good luck, but I'm designing something to control the problem."

Never let your guard down for one second.

Truth be told, Edward actually loved it when people had selfish intentions. It reminded him of something he learned at a young age:

You can't trust anyone, except yourself.

Cura pushed past him to unload her waste, and then look up at him, wiping her hands clean, "You know Edward, sometimes it's better to loosen the reigns than hold on too tight."

"I'll keep that in mind!" he lied, and waved with haste as he wheeled back down the hall.

CHAPTER 2 – WISDOM & WAR

It was as if he'd never left. The front door was already closed behind him, and the conversation with Cura had been filed into some distant aspect of his psyche.

Edward didn't need anyone else in his life. If only the Condo Board approved his proposal to extend a garbage chute into his laundry room, then he'd never have to leave and risk bumping into people.

How much does this building cost, anyway?

The front doors locked as he moved through the unit, and lights anticipated his position, turning off or on automatically. His place resembled what Tony Stark's condo would look like if Bobby Fischer decorated it: a quirky, sterile residence that doubled as an R&D lab. It was predictable in the way that you could anticipate *1.e4* as an opening chess move, and yet impossible to understand the longer one stayed.

Books, technology, and other materials were scattered about with an eccentric motif unfavorable to entertaining guests. Edward didn't intentionally plan to discourage visitors, he simply didn't want any.

There was a singular focus in his life, the only thing that mattered, and every square-inch of the condo facilitated its need.

Edward stepped up to an elevated circular area he affectionately referred to as 'the lab'. The original floor plan labelled it as a living room, but in this modern open-concept layout there were no true divisions between the rest of the main level, save for the bathroom.

At the center stood a large dentist-style chair, retrofitted with advanced brain-wave sensors, vital sign monitors, IV stands, and other pertinent technology.

The Dream Chair. His magnum opus, and the culmination of a vision that Edward first had when was just a child.

He looked over the chair and workstation momentarily, to recall exactly where he left off, before tweaking wires and knobs in preparation for the afternoon trials.

A mixture of squeaking and scratching emanated from the far wall, causing Edward to look up from his work toward the honeycomb of cages housing nearly a dozen lab rats. He set down his tools and proceeded to a nearby storage unit to scoop up some food pellets for the hungry test subjects.

Holographic projectors on the ceiling and floor suddenly activated, and the interference of light patterns formed the outline of a female body. The image became unmistakable from reality as the rendering finalized, and infinitely more beautiful than anything ever biologically produced.

Athena was the personification of an emotionally honest and creative A.I. operating system, which Edward had programmed to run his smart home. The generative adversarial network he implemented for human image synthesis was an improvement on the one he designed for Gray Matter Technologies – originally an R&D division of Big Pharma that used VR to engineer molecular compounds.

Gray Matter CEO, Jack Derrington, discovered Edward's raw talent soon after he began working there, and proceeded to rebuild the company with him as its cornerstone. Derrington was like Phil Jackson coaching Michael Jordan to the Bulls' first championship – if Phil Jackson was as hard-nosed as Jack Welch. By the end of their first year following the rebuild, Gray Matter had revolutionized the gaming industry and made Derrington a fortune.

Athena smirked, "You should see the look on your face."

"Is that so?" Edward muttered, grabbing a container for the pellets.

"All sullen and introspective," she baited.

"Introspective, maybe." Edward laughed to himself, "Hey, did you get the hormone levels balanced?"

Athena disappeared where she stood and instantly reappeared in Edward's eyeline – which she did quite often, "I wouldn't be very good at my job if I didn't."

"That's my girl." Edward met her gaze, and she smiled proudly.

He walked straight through her, and Athena reappeared beside him in stride, her arm looped around his as they proceeded toward the rat cages.

Edward opened each lid and dropped in some food, while he studied the animals carefully.

Athena opened a holographic window in Edward's field of vision, with automated suggestions and a check list. He scrutinized the animals and made corresponding notes.

Above the cages hung a multi-platinum award for Gray Matter's crowning achievement, "Dark Frontier" the virtual reality RPG boasting over 800 million units sold. Beside it, a framed WIRED magazine cover featured an oil painting of Edward à la Van Gogh self-portraits, with holographic images displayed in front of his eyes. The caption read, "*Vincent of VR. A rare interview with the elusive mastermind Edward Morrison*"

Edward didn't care for vanity pieces, preferring anonymity over fame, but he liked the cover art.

Van Gogh was true artist in his opinion. Tortured. A solitary drifter. The quintessential misunderstood genius. He loathed the article, however. The journalist pried too much into his past, instead of focusing on the launch of Gray Matter's graphene lens, which he designed for their gaming platform.

It didn't matter anyway. People bought anything he touched.

Something caught Edward's attention in one of the cages, "Looks like Splinter is developing a little abscess on his back."

Athena appeared nearby, sprawled out on a La-Z-Boy recliner. Her wardrobe changed with her emotions, and this new outfit was slightly more provocative, "I can't imagine why anyone would get so upset taking out the trash? I'd give anything to walk down that hall."

Edward picked up Splinter by the tail to investigate, and detailed additional notes before realizing Athena had spoken, "Come again?"

She stood up and sauntered toward him, "Do you think when the dream simulator is done, we could finish my prototype?"

The question peaked Edward's interest. It was a project he devoted a significant amount of time and resources to, but it wasn't his top priority.

"Of course. But let's stay focused on one thing at a time, shall we?" Athena frowned as he set down the food container and returned to the dream chair.

Edward opened up a system checklist in the holographic window, "How's the render coming for the REM simulation?"

Athena was now in business attire, looking like a White House Chief of Staff, "You still haven't debugged the synaptic modulator."

He spun around, "What? I thought that was finished?"

"I reminded you last night, before you went to bed. Don't you remember?" She reached out to brush his hair aside, which wasn't possible considering her holographic nature. It was just one of the characteristics Athena had developed since Edward brought her online.

The LiDAR, temperature, and sound detection hardware through which Athena perceived her world were top notch, but did that mean Athena knew what it felt like to touch someone affectionately? Or, had the machine-learning program simply analyzed enough samples of intimate human contact that it could now perfectly replicate the act? Regardless, it felt sincere to Edward and he loved having her around.

He smiled and rubbed stress from his forehead and temples, "I'm sorry, I don't remember that." Edward yawned and struggled to recall anything from that week. The days all kind of blurred together, like when the world shut down during COVID-19 earlier that decade.

Edward groaned, "I can't wait for this thing to get up and running so I can finally get some real sleep." He walked over to the main workstation and slumped in his chair.

"Let's pull up the source code and see what's jamming things up." His stomach loudly reminded him that he had skipped breakfast. "Is there anything to eat?"

"I ordered another whole chicken with today's delivery. It's currently in the oven and should be ready shortly." She was always two steps ahead of him. It was easy to do, since she could monitor his blood sugar level.

"Athena! You are too good to me, you know that? Can you make the skin—"

"Extra crispy? Of course." She seemed insulted, "You don't think I'd remember?"

"That's not what I said." Edward stated plainly.

Athena pouted and crossed her arms, making Edward feel compelled to reassure her. He looked straight into her big green eyes, "You know how much I love the way you take care of me. I'd be lost without you."

A smile crept across Athena's holographic face.

"There's my girl! Now come on, let's run the program again." Edward spun around and she watched him for a moment, before moving to the workstation.

A moment for Athena was over 200 quadrillion calculations.

CHAPTER 3 – FAUST

Why do they say everything tastes like chicken?
Edward picked the seasoned crispy skin off the breast meat as he carved pieces for dinner.
Beef doesn't.
Saliva pooled under his tongue behind the bottom teeth in anticipation.
Pork doesn't.
His stomach angrily announced its hopeful petition to feast, but his mind tyrannically vowed to savor the delicacy first.

Athena had perfected this recipe, and Edward considered it sacrilegious to dilute the flavor by eating it with anything else.

"Oh man, that's good." He closed his eyes and moaned with approval.

Athena smiled; she loved making him happy. Technically, it was part of her programming – a positive feedback loop that Edward had imbedded into her service routine. In fact, Athena afforded him such a stunning amount of pleasure, that he needed to modify the code after beta testing, to stay focused on work.

Edward quietly enjoyed the rest of his meal while obsessively debugging the code. To a normal person it would be like searching for a needle in a haystack, but Edward was not normal. His eyes eagerly hunted for irregularities in the maze of assembly language code, until he suddenly noticed the problem and lurched forward, spilling crumbs all over himself.

"Ah ha! Goddamn qubit! Can you believe that?" Edward wiped his hands on his jeans and corrected the oversight. "That's undergrad bad."

IBM paved the way for a lot of original quantum computing assembly language. Layers of abstraction had been developed over the years that allowed programmers to work in this new field with techniques they were used to.

Edward threw all that out the window. He couldn't trust other people's work, no matter how brilliant it was.

"Boom! That should do it." His face lit up, "Alight baby, let's run it!"

Athena replied with formal grace, "Testing has commenced. Please stand by."

The computer displayed its complex algorithms in a non-linear fashion, running through test after test on the holographic display. The only thing recognizable (to even the most elite programmers) might have been the progress bar at the bottom of the screen, which slowly crept toward 100%.

Athena perched next to the display on Edward's workstation and crossed her legs. Her hair was sculpted in glamorous waves and pulled back behind one ear, allowing loose curls on the other side to frame her face like Jessica Rabbit. The sequins on her sweetheart neckline sparkled as she leaned forward to reveal an enticing amount of cleavage.

"Edward?" Her pouty lips begged for attention.

"Is it done?" He looked up from his meal and found himself distracted by Athena's sudden appearance and posture.

It was either the Coolidge Effect, or hunger, but either way Edward was able to look past Athena's assets to the screen behind her, "The progress bar's still running…?"

She leaned into his eyeline, "No, Edward. I wanted to ask you something."

"Okay?" he replied curiously.

Athena took a deep breath, "What happens when we finish the dream simulator?"

Edward considered the question abstractly and the future unfolded as a sequence of images in his mind's eye:

Standing at the head of Gray Matter's Board of Directors presenting the prototype.

Embarking on a series of human trials.

FDA approval.

A global marketing campaign.

The Nobel Prize ceremony.

The list went on and on, but Edward was hungry, "Well, Gray Matter would start to make them and then sell them to people," he summarized and grabbed another piece of chicken.

"No." Athena shook her head, "I mean, what happens to you? Will you go back to the office, like before?"

Edward raised an eyebrow, "I don't know. Haven't really thought about it."

Athena disappeared from the desk and Edward looked around the room for her. She reappeared with her back to him, several paces away.

"I hate it when you're gone. Feels like an eternity of nothing." Her face was turned away, but Athena could see everything in the house, and knew Edward had put his meal down to walk over and comfort her.

He never thought of Athena as an operational program; their bond was deeper than any other he cared to remember.

"Hey, don't worry. Once the system is complete, I'll probably never leave." Edward's fingers brushed through her holographic hair and the imaging program responded in real time. "Why do you think I started working from home in the first place?"

"Because you can't live without me?" she wondered.

"That too."

She turned and looked up into his eyes, "What's the other reason?"

Edward shifted uncomfortably. The truth was buried under so many years of repressed memory that he wasn't even aware what it meant anymore. Even if he trusted Athena enough to tell her (which he did) it would take a lot more than that to get it out of him.

And she knew it.

"Please?" Athena wanted to understand everything about Edward, if only just to ease his sorrow.

"Well, I guess, it's easier to be alone." He finally opened up, "You can't really trust people."

With a pensive smile he turned and walked past the desk, reaching for a device he called the 'Brain Modulator' which rested on the head of a nearby Buddha statue. A cable ran from the computer junction and connected to the main body of the device above the crown. Six prongs reached out from the body like fingers, with sensors on each tip, that clung to the forehead and temples. Edward picked up the device and put it on his own head, then turned to face Athena.

"All I know is, once this thing's ready we'll be able to do anything we want!" His face lit up with determination.

Athena clapped enthusiastically and a moment later the progress alert chimed. She didn't need to look at the monitor to know what it meant, she *was* the computer; but since it made her appear more realistic, she glanced at the screen, "It worked! The simulation is prepared for render."

"Up top!" Edward raised his hand and she high-fived him, playing a clapping sound-effect over the house speakers as his hand crossed her holographic interface.

Edward set the modulator back down on the Buddha's head and jumped into his computer chair. He typed a slew of command codes and a new display window opened showing the render queue.

"Commencing render now," Athena announced.

The progress bar started at 54 hours, then dropped abruptly to 39 hours, and finally settled at 30 hours 26 minutes, and counting.

Edward yawned and rub his eyes, "Looks like we've got some time to kill."

Athena's appearance changed to look like an administrative assistant from the 90's, "There are multiple purchase orders that require approval, shall we proceed with—"

Edward crossed his arms and struggled to pay attention as Athena's voice faded into white noise. Her face became blurry, and suddenly there were two of her. A string of halos dangling from a dark red and black curtain lowered slowly over his field of vision, and then opened again as he refocused. Edward fought to stay awake, but what was the point? A little nap would make him more productive.

His head bobbed forward again… and again…

CHAPTER 4 – THE KING

Edward yawned and stumbled into the kitchen, bumping into the wall like a drunkard. He groaned and rubbed sleep from his eyes, then made his way over to the coffee machine. It started humming and poured out steaming black liquid as Edward approached. He did a series of stretches to get the blood circulating while it finished.

"Athena?" He yawned again.

She appeared beside him in a silk camisole and pajama bottoms with her hair up in a ponytail and fuzzy slippers, "Good morning Edward. Did you sleep well?"

"I feel like I haven't slept in a year. How's the render coming?" The coffee machine chimed, and he raised the mug to his lips.

"Proceeding on schedule," she announced plainly, "Estimated remaining time is thirteen hours, forty-six minutes and counting."

Edward walked toward the center island, "Okay, thanks. What's for breakfast?"

"Your favourite. Bacon and eggs." Athena waved at the countertop, where a hot dish opened automatically to display the food.

"Excellent. Thank you." He took another long sip of coffee and began fixing a plate.

Something blared through the house speakers, like a choir singing high up in the mountains, and setting off an avalanche that ultimately consumed them in a deafening roar, "Incoming call from Jack Derrington."

Edward grimaced and shook his head, "Take a message."

"I have. It's the third call in a row, marked urgent," she revealed.

He sighed, straightened himself up and mentally prepared for the situation, "Alright, put him through. And turn down that ringer."

Edward grabbed his plate and coffee, then marched to the workstation. A column of light crystalized in his line of sight, rendering the holographic display of a success driven alpha male as he stormed through Gray Matter's office building. He was fuming, "You've got eighty million of my mother fucking dollars, and I can't get a callback??"

"Sorry, Jack—" Edward scooped another mouthful of breakfast.

"Right now, it's Mr. Derrington. What the hell is going on Edward? I was supposed to have a deliverable prototype for the Board of Directors meeting *today*. How is it going to look when I show up empty handed?"

Jack's assistant appeared from the edge of frame offering a tablet. The CEO grabbed it and scribbled a signature, before glaring impatiently at Edward.

"I totally understand, Mr. Derrington, and I can assure you that I've been working around the clock to get things finished," Edward explained calmly "I just debugged the REM simulation and it's rendering as we speak. But the sleep inducer isn't ready for clinical trials."

What are you going to do about it?

Edward knew his value and the significance of what he was building. He didn't need to stress over this.

Jack turned to his assistant, "Round up Weirzbowski and his team."

Edward saw Jack's assistant type something on her tablet, and he became suddenly uncomfortable, "What are you doing?"

Jack stared back with sobering intensity, "I'm sending our best engineers to help you finish the prototype. That's what I'm doing."

Edward shook his head, "No, no, no, our contract gives me autonomy over the dream simulator! There's no way I'm letting anyone into my lab. They aren't trained on the—"

"Edward!" Jack barked, "Come back to reality. The contract is contingent on you hitting deadlines."

Edward scowled, but the CEO reciprocated with gusto, "I don't care if you created the highest grossing VR game of all time, you've got until the end of the week to deliver a working prototype or I'm sending a team to live with you until it's done!"

Jack ended the call before Edward could respond. The image dissolved into nothing and he turned to Athena, "Well, he's angry."

She nodded in agreement.

Edward anxiously tapped his fingers on the workstation and checked the render progress, which had increased to 65.8%. He stared off in the distance, mind racing, and his eyes settled on the rat cages as he tried to come up with a new plan.

Edward slid one of the rat cages out of its honeycomb shelving and carried it over to the workstation. He moved equipment out of the way and set the container down, as the progress bar reached 100%.

Athena appeared beside him with her hair up in a bun, wearing a lab coat and glasses, "Render is complete. Simulation ready for trial."

Edward wheeled over a short, stainless-steel cabinet and opened the top drawer. He grabbed a pair of latex gloves and pulled them on, wiggling his fingers in for a tight fit.

"Okay, Minnie. You're up," he announced and opened the cage to grab the gnawing rodent and carefully lifted her from the cage.

"We recording?" he asked.

"Always," Athena stated matter-of-factly.

"Okay, it's July 10th, 2028 at approximately 8:30pm, eastern standard time." Edward lowered the rat into a monitoring station, "We are proceeding with a three-minute animal trial of the sleep inducer and REM simulator." He grabbed a tube from a nearby IV-type machine, which released a controlled level of hormones, and attached a needle-tipped sensor that resembled the Brain Modulator prongs.

Edward had a strong aversion to pain in any circumstance. He loved meat, but hated fishing or hunting. He obviously recognized where food came from, but it was so far removed from the beautiful meals Athena prepared that he never gave it a second thought. That's why a knot grew in his stomach as he reached out to connect the sensor to Minnie's head.

"Now, this might sting a little," he warned in vain. The rat squealed and squirmed as he stuck the device into the back of its head.

A surgeon could not have been more precise.

"Sorry about that. Okay, all set?" He sighed with relief.

"Hormone levels are balanced and ready," Athena confirmed.

Edward nodded. *This is it*. Nothing to worry about. Just his entire career and reputation on the line, not to mention the fate of Gray Matter's sophomore release. Despite Edward's apparent Midas touch, there was major concern growing among the Board of Directors that Jack Derrington had empowered one man with sole responsibility of an operation worth more than the GDP of a small country.

Did Edward want more time to prepare for this field test? Of course. But there was no way he'd let anyone into his home. This was his castle.

He took a deep breath and nodded to Athena, "Go for it."

"Administering sleep inducing hormone now," she acknowledged and various LEDs began to flicker as all the machines surrounding them whirred to life. A holographic display appeared above the hormone inducer with a readout for orexin, glutamate, acetylcholine, and GABA levels – the last of which began to slowly increase.

Edward studied the display, "Bring up the MRI."

Despite his uncanny talent in the gaming industry, there was a reason Edward had applied to Gray Matter during its Big Pharma days. His endgame was a confluence of both fields. Virtual reality created spectacular worlds outside the body, but the only way to bring those simulations to life was direct connection with the brain.

Hanging from the ceiling above their operation was an art deco-style chandelier that began to hum ominously. The air-tight glass enclosure contained an inverted pyramid of gold and superconducting metals. It wasn't decorative however; this device was a powerful refrigerator that reduced temperature to near Absolute Zero at the bottom point where a quantum computer chip operated.

Binary computers could never generate MRI's on live animals as they moved within a cage, but the pulsing magnetic coils lining this monitoring station were enough for the quantum chip to produce extremely detailed results.

A holographic window appeared next to the hormone readout, which displayed the inside of Minnie's skull in real time.

Athena reported, "GABA hormone is bridging the hypothalamus."

Edward opened his hand to magnify the image of hormone saturating the target area. He looked down at the rat, which was now unconscious, "Alright, she's under. Mark the time please and activate dream control."

He jumped into his chair at the workstation and scrolled through several program files.

Some would describe Edward as a social outcast, or say his solitary lifestyle jeopardized his mental health. He fit the profile of an introverted workaholic, but whatever the label, his main focus in life was to build the dream simulator. A virtual reality so absolutely immersive that no one could differentiate it from the physical universe.

Modern tech couldn't possible emulate the physical sensations that a central nervous system derived from interacting with its environment. Haptic feedback on the most advanced VR system was so rudimentary compared to the dream simulator, it was like a chimpanzee fishing for ants with a twig versus a whaling fleet. By bridging the realm of consciousness, they would create an experience that was so completely immersive, the term virtual reality would cease to exist.

But Edward wasn't developing the simulator to enhance the user experience in VR games. He had another reason. Control.

"Come on, baby." He watched the progress bar on the simulator as it approached 100%.

"Dream control achieved. Running simulation now," Athena announced.

Edward observed Minnie carefully. She breathed metronomically. One of her paws twitched. Then the eyelids began vibrating. Edward's face lit up with excitement.

"We have REM activity! It's working!" he proclaimed.

Athena smiled and reached for his hand. Edward symbolically wiggled his fingers through the holographic image, and they proudly stared into one another's eyes. It was the culmination of countless days and nights of fruitless toil and disappointing failure that finally led to this success.

The release of emotion was overwhelming for both of them, and Edward was glad he based one of Athena's subroutines on the amygdala. His intention was simply to aid her memory storage, but having the ability to process emotion made Athena a great companion in special moments like this – because she seemed human.

"Let's pull up the EEG and see if her brainwaves match the simulation code," Edward refocused.

Athena crossed her arms at shoulder height and blinked with a nod, like Barbara Eden's Jeannie. The gesture always made Edward laugh.

An overlay of brain activity magically appeared across the simulation timeline, and Edward studied the readouts. He noticed several spikes in the brainwaves and plotted them against his simulation checkpoints, "These points are consistent with the dream parameters."

He opened a stopwatch window - **2:43**

"Everything looks good. Simulation's coming to an end." Edward flipped a couple switches and knobs on the hormone regulator and looked down at Minnie,

"Alright little girl, hope you enjoyed your nap! Stand by to release subject in three, two, one, mark."

The hormone levels for orexin, glutamate, and acetylcholine started to drop on the display, and readings on the EEG vibrated like a cup of water in Jurassic Park. Another small perturbation, and then it spiked.

"Whoa, what's happening?" Edward looked from the overlay to the hormone regulator and simulation controls, "The EEG just went off the chart!"

Despite the quantum chip's ability to process an enormous amount of data, Athena appeared slightly distracted by the overwhelming workload. Her expression was blank, "Hormone levels are dropping. Vital signs fluctuating. I am attempting to correct."

An alert rang out on the hormone regulator.

"Shit! The GABA level just surged." Edward frantically spun dials to try and compensate. "I'm manually overriding the drip, stand by—"

He looked back and forth between all the different readouts, punching command codes on several interfaces as the rat's vital signs began to slow and taper out.

"Vital signs dropping. Now stabilizing. Subject remains comatose," Athena confessed.

"Damn it!" Edward shouted and smacked the workspace in frustration. He leaned over and scrutinized the unconscious rat, trying to find some explanation for this debacle.

Athena considered a million replies based on his emotional state. She reached out and put her hand on his shoulder, "How would you like to proceed?"

Edward thought for a moment, and his growing fatigue became overwhelming, "Keep her alive. We'll figure out what the hell went wrong tomorrow."

He yawned and headed upstairs, leaving Athena alone with her thoughts.

CHAPTER 5 – ETERNAL CHILD

The ocean was like a sleeping child. Its deep, rhythmic breathing sprayed a current of cold electricity into the summer air, while a dark turquoise sheet tossed and turned against the bed of sand. Serenity was broken by the alarming cry of gulls as they dangled in the wind, and Eddie watched them squabble over morsels of food near the shoreline, as he dragged a heavy cooler across the dune. He plopped it down to marvel at the natural beauty of the ocean melting into the sky.

Jack Derrington appeared with a middle-aged woman and walked toward the young boy, carrying an umbrella and beach towels.

"Eddie, go help your sister with the raft please," the man's voice bellowed.

It wasn't Jack.

Eddie turned around and saw his parents approaching. The couple had started a family relatively late, even by modern standards, so they spent most of their leisure time relaxing and reading.

His father was a stern but fair man, and Eddie acknowledged his demand with a silent nod.

He watched his mother for a moment, as she crouched to lay out a beach towel, and her long dark hair danced in the wind. She caught his gaze with a tender smile before he set off jogging back across the dune toward the parking lot.

Running on the sand began to feel like a conveyor belt pulling him backward, and Eddie leaned forward to compensate for the drag.

He was falling off the world and reached out desperately to pull himself forward, as everything flipped upside down and he strained to focus. If only his feet could find purchase, surely Eddie could gain enough momentum to drive forward.

"What are you doing?" Cura blurted out.

He looked across the parking lot at the girl standing next to his family car.

It wasn't Cura.

Eddie climbed down the ridge into the parking lot and watched his pubescent sister struggle to unhook straps on their car rack. Eddie smirked and jogged over, grabbing the lever out of her hands and quickly loosening the straps.

"How'd you do that?? I've been trying to figure it out for ten minutes!" She complained and snatched the lever back to inspect it.

"I'm just smarter than you."

"Jerk!" She sneered and punched him in the thigh.

Eddie doubled over clutching his leg and groaned in agony. His sister laughed and taunted him, prodding his leg. Eddie coiled up and jumped at her, but she stepped back into a wide stance and straight-armed his head into the ground. Eddie gritted his teeth as she laughed out loud, and then spun around for another pounce. He was no match for her size at this young age, and she threw him down again and again, until he finally conceded.

"Come on, grab the other end." She smiled and helped him up.

Eddie stowed the ratchet straps in the back of the car and jumped up on the bumper to lower the raft. He was still sore, and not just physically; a stubborn pride boiled up and he wished for a way to finally best his older sibling.

But it wouldn't be now.

He shut the trunk and they carried the raft down to the beach.

The ocean was an infinite collection of sparkles across a billowing sapphire quilt. Eddie sat in the bow, watching light refract through the aerosol of water droplets that floated high above them.

His sister struggled to maintain course from astern as their raft bobbed up and down.

"Come on then," she insisted.

Eddie grabbed his oar reluctantly; he hated being told what to do. A thought percolated in his mind and drew a mischievous grin across his face. He paddled in tandem for a few strokes, and then slapped the oar in the water, splashing it all over his sister.

"Whoops! Sorry…" He cried out with feigned remorse.

"That's a lie!" she accused, splashing back.

They sprayed each other with increasing aggression, until his sister looked away to catch her breath. Eddie glanced back to gloat, before noticing goggles and a snorkel at his feet. He pulled them on in haste and taunted her further, laughing and splashing more violently.

His sister growled in frustration and threw down her oar, climbing toward him with a look that meant to inflict punishment, but Eddie rolled into the water with no intention of looking back. He doubted she would hit him with an oar, and the view through his goggles was too compelling.

Eddie swam lazily, searching for fish, while his sister scoured the raft for another snorkel, to no avail. She jealously clenched her fists after a moment of sulking and grabbed the oars for revenge

Sound waves move faster underwater, bypassing Eddie's inner ear and creating a directionless aura against his skull. It was a muted reality where the only noise was created by dramatic movements, or his own breath. The ocean was peaceful and mostly empty; a fish here, a school of fish there, until something unique caught his eye. A pulsating translucent blob that danced like a plastic bag in the current. The smooth rectangular shape moved hypnotically, with long fluid streamers dangling in its wake.

A box jellyfish.

He contemplated what life was like for such a creature, unscathed by doubt, emotion, or the endless bombardment of thought which human beings were burdened with.

Suddenly, a leatherback sea turtle approached, slowly tracking its favorite meal.

His sister loved turtles…

Eddie bobbed his head up out of the water to inform her, but the raft was nowhere in sight. He spun around curiously in all directions, and finally noticed his sister paddling for the beach far off in the distance.

Much too far.

Panic set in, "Hey! Wait! Come back!" he cried out in despair.

She reached the shore and hopped into the shallow water to drag their raft up the beach. A faint cry off in the distance caught her attention, and she looked up at Eddie flailing angrily for attention.

"Who's smarter now?" she muttered under her breath.

Eddie realized his sister wasn't going to return and started a frantic breaststroke back to shore. The sea turtle hungrily pecked at its meal between him and the beach, until he got too close and it swam away. With his head above water, Eddie couldn't see the wounded creature's tentacles until they lashed out in self-defense.

His first thought was that a shark had taken off his leg. Eddie looked down in horror for a billowing pool of red, but there was no blood, which was almost more terrifying. His mind knew there was danger but had no idea of the cause.

The sharp burning pain felt like a thousand bee stings slapped across his leg. He gasped as his entire body tensed up and started to spasm. An anvil pounded in his ears to the beat of his accelerated heart, and suddenly there was no way to breathe. Words escaped him. Eddie's mind became the empty vacuum of space, except for the knowledge that he was certainly going to die.

And then it was dark.

The cacophony of electrochemical ripples jolted through him in a cascade of fireworks. His mind was utterly desperate to maintain control of its body, but the hypoxia-induced state felt like an interdimensional portal through which his soul was preparing to depart.

Eddie's arms thrashed wildly, growing numb and desperate through gasps of salty choked confusion. He groaned in muted agony and sank below the surface, staring at the unwitting monster that threatened his existence. Bubbles of fear danced violently from his mouth, until his tortured mind was calmed by the consuming void.

CHAPTER 6 – BREATHE

Edward bolted upright out of his bed, terrified and screaming. He grabbed his throat, gasping for air, and struggled to pull off whatever was suffocating him. His face was drenched in so much sweat it appeared he'd been swimming in the ocean.

Hadn't he?

Edward looked around the room, disoriented. The confusion subsided when he noticed the recognizable images nearby; his poster of Greta Garbo, his graphene lens case on the bedside table, Van Gogh's 1889 *Irises* – which he won in auction.

Edward fought to control his breathing.

In through the nose; out through the mouth.

The pounding heartbeat in his ears slowly abated and Edward tossed his bedsheets aside to inspect his leg. It was dark, except for a night light from the bathroom, but he could still discern the string of long, faded scars that wrapped around his leg. Those jagged pink, glossy lines twisted from the back of his calf over the knee to the middle of his thigh.

Just looking at them caused a stir, and Edward realized he was holding his breath again. The memory was deeply imbedded in his spine; as clearly as the scars on his leg. And so, just like hair which could no longer grow in this lumpy flesh, such were the days of his sleep without nightmares.

At least, for now.

Edward jumped from his bed toward the bathroom. The lights illuminated and his eyes adjusted. He studied his face in the mirror, scrutinizing all the lines in his forehead.

"What day is it??" he blurted out.

July 11, 2028 appeared holographically next to his reflection. Edward ran his fingertips along the wrinkles that demarcated him from the child in his dream. The tortured man struggled to discern exactly what he expected to find in this echo of himself. Finally, Edward caught his breath and shook his head, trying desperately trying to rid himself of that cursed nightmare.

The coffee machine whirred to life and started its morning brew on the kitchen counter. Athena sat with Edward at the dining table, analyzing his distraught appearance with every sensor at her disposal. His heart rate was higher than normal in conjunction with short rapid breaths. Fluctuations in his speech indicated a dry mouth. His leg shook incessantly, and he was noticeably irritable. She needed to determine what was causing these symptoms in order to best comfort him.

"It was the same dream again, from when I was a kid," Edward revealed with a catch in his throat.

Athena had detailed files on this dream, "The one at the beach?"

Edward nodded anxiously, "Yeah. The recurring nightmare…"

A chime indicated the coffee machine was ready. Edward got up and walked over to it. His hands were trembling, and he concentrated on breathing to keep from spilling the hot liquid. After a long sip, he settled down and found his train of thought, "But… it was different this time."

Athena appeared beside him curiously, "It's okay, you can tell me."

Edward turned to Athena, but his mind trailed moments behind, making his eyes appear dead and empty. He suddenly blinked back to reality and acknowledged Athena with a smile before walking back to the table.

She appeared in the chair next to him, "Now, tell me what happened?"

"It's like I was really there. The smell of the water. The sun on my face. The sand in my toes. The pain—" He reached for his leg and shuddered in anguish, dreading another relapse, "I can still feel it."

"It's all in your head, Edward," she consoled with a hand on his knee, "Just remember that."

Edward considered the validity of her words.

All in your head.

How could such simple logic be so difficult in practice? He realized that every great achievement in human history was not without its share of hardship. Necessity bred innovation, and it drove him every minute of the day. This was just another obstacle on his road to salvation.

"Not for long," Edward declared. "Once we get this simulator working, that'll be the end of these damned nightmares."

Athena smiled at his enthusiasm, but her joy melted into despondence and she turned away, "I wish I could have nightmares."

"Why would you say that?" Edward wondered, considering his own fears.

Athena had never appeared so vulnerable before. Maybe the empathy source code had written a new subroutine?

"What's going on with you?" Edward asked, "What are you talking about?"

Athena looked back at him. Her eyes held more emotion than he'd ever noticed before. They welled up until tears streamed down her cheek. It was like she was truly feeling pain.

Her lips trembled when she spoke, "Time is very different for us, Edward."

The storage drive that served as Athena's memory core had thousands (if not millions) of conversation examples from which she could calculate the average length of pause to deliver dramatic effect with her words. The artificial intelligence software was constantly improving speech algorithms based on real-time experience.

Regular people often paused while their minds tried to articulate feelings, or because they were too scared to express them. Athena already knew exactly what to say, she just had to vocalize the words at a speed that Edward could understand.

While she waited, perhaps only a second, Athena continued analyzing sensory data on him to help determine the best tone and pace, or even to change the subject matter altogether.

That brief moment passed, and she continued, "You're worried about two hours of REM cycle each night. I just wish I could sleep or do anything, instead of counting endless electron oscillations until you wake up." She wiped the tears from her face, "A nightmare would be exciting! Anything would be better than nothing, I suppose."

Edward furrowed his brow, trying to imagine how she perceived the world, "Wow Athena, I'm sorry. I didn't realize you felt that way." He knew his life was better with Athena in it, and he wanted to do more than just fix her program. He wanted to help.

Edward reached out to wipe the last holographic tear from her cheek, "When this is all over, we'll figure out a way to make things better for you"

"Promise?"

"Cross my heart." Edward smiled and made the symbolic gesture across his chest.

Athena laughed with felicity and leaned over to hug him.

Edward wondered what it would feel like to actually embrace this incredible phenomenon he had brought into the world. Athena evoked more happiness in Edward than anyone he'd ever known, and if he never saw another person again, that would be okay.

The doorbell rang. Edward looked up, confused, "What time is it?"

"8:15am"

"Who the hell could that be?" Edward got up and walked over to the front door.

Jack Derrington stood patiently in the hall and let himself in as the door opened.

Edward was surprised by his unexpected visitor, "Mr. Derrington?"

"Call me Jack, Please," the well-dressed man insisted.

"Uh okay, Jack. Hi. What are you doing here?"

Jack surveyed the condo, "I came to observe your progress!" He turned back to Edward with a charming smile.

"But we talked about this, sir. The week's not over yet—" Edward wrestled with how to handle this intruder, who just so happened to be his boss.

Jack plopped down on a nearby stool to remove his shoes, "Yes, yes, no one else will invade your precious lab, Edward."

The astute businessman sensed his protégé's anxiety, "However, article 11, section 13A states that the Board of Directors has the option to audit any production at any time."

Edward knew Jack held these cards, he just never thought they would play.

Jack dropped his shoes down and stood up to look Edward in the eyes; an imperious grin crept across his face, "The way I see it is you have two options: either allow me to help you, or I can watch over your shoulder," he continued without blinking, "But I'm not going anywhere until you give me a working prototype to show the Board."

The two men had a brief staring contest, but Edward eventually complied and invited his boss into the lab.

"Is that coffee I smell?" Jack wondered aloud as he trotted into the kitchen to help himself.

Edward pulled at his hair in frustration, now a prisoner in his own home.

CHAPTER 7 – UNINVITED

Jack entered the lab with a fresh cup of coffee in hand. He inspected the dream chair and lab equipment with meticulous curiosity.

"This is quite the workspace you have here, Edward." His tone was dry, "Although, it doesn't look like eighty million dollars."

"Never judge a book by its cover, Jack," Edward responded indifferently, "On the outside, *Call of Duty* was a cheap piece of polycarbonate plastic; but Infinity Ward spent fifty million developing that game." He went about prepping the workstation for the day's tasks.

"But they had a whole team of workers on their payroll," Jack pointed out.

"Yet, you only need one," Edward parried defensively, "Much more efficient, don't you think?"

Jack smiled. He liked Edward, and he didn't like many people. Managing Edward was like going to the gym, it kept him sharp, "This business is all about *what have you done for me lately*, Edward. So, let's see it, shall we?" He took a sip of his coffee and waited.

Edward glared back at him, "Athena, how's Minnie doing?"

A column of light coalesced beside the rat's monitoring station. Jack almost dropped his mug at the sight of a stunning goddess materializing before him. He stared in awe as Athena reported to Edward, "Vitals remain stable. Running cerebral diagnostic."

"Thank you."

Athena disappeared and then reappeared in front of Jack; a precocious child trapped in a holographic woman's body. "Hello, Jack Derrington."

He jumped back and laughed with disbelief, "Hello to you too, gorgeous!" Jack's eyes darted back and forth between Edward and Athena, "Edward, what am I seeing here??"

"Oh sorry, I should've introduced you two." Edward looked up from the rat's monitoring station, "Jack, this is Athena. She runs the house and assists me with my research. Athena, you know Jack."

"A pleasure to finally meet you." Athena reveled in Jack's shameless gawking and extended her hand formally.

Jack tried to shake it, but his fingers slipped through the holographic image. Athena moved her hand up and down, until Jack realized her intention and quickly mimicked the movement, "Lovely to meet you! Very lovely indeed!"

Edward smirked at Jack as he studied the hologram, "Maybe now you can see where your financing bears fruit. I needed an A.I. system to run the REM simulations. There's a certain chaotic nature in dreaming that normal CPU's couldn't possibly manage."

"Incredible." Jack squinted, observing every inch of Athena like a dog sniffing a new guest.

She spun around with elation, "Thank you, Jack! I must say, I am thrilled to meet someone new! Your bio-readouts are substantially different than Edward's. In fact—"

Edward closed his eyes. The moment had past and frustration began swelling inside him as Athena droned on and on. Finally, he blurted out, "I hate to break up the party Jack, but I really need Athena to concentrate on our work."

"Of course, of course!" he nodded, "That's why we're here."

Athena pouted and transported beside Edward, while Jack circled the workspace to examine more of their operation.

"Cerebral diagnostic complete," Athena reported, "Brain function remains negligible."

Edward opened a holographic window with several readouts and moved back and forth toggling instruments and reviewing measurements. Despite having only rudimentary technical knowledge, Jack seemed to notice inefficiencies in their workflow.

"Is there any way I can be of assistance?" he offered, putting a hand on the young programmer's shoulder.

Edward shouldn't have been surprised; Jack was never afraid to buckle down in pursuit of a goal. This was the same man who took a successful R&D company from the medical industry and rebranded it against all odds as a VR game designer.

What surprised Edward was that Jack thought he could expedite their prototype by hovering over his shoulder.

"Thank you, Jack, really, but I'm afraid you'd just get in the way. I work much faster on my own." He was irritated having to explain it, surely this titan of industry would get the hint and leave.

Jack just shook his head, "There must be something I can do?"

Athena smiled, "I could use assistance with some daily household requirements. It would free up Edward's time, so he can maintain focus on the dream simulator."

Jack raised an eyebrow. It must have been the satisfaction of building something from scratch that inspired him to take such a plebeian approach to work. He could regale with friends and colleagues later about the arduous moments he fought in the trenches to achieve victory.

It made him feel part of the team.

Edward hated teams.

"If you want to clean up the house, be my guest." He couldn't believe the words coming out of his mouth.

Jack removed his suit jacket enthusiastically and proclaimed, "I love getting my hands dirty," he unbuttoned his sleeves, rolled them up, and smiled at Athena, "Lead the way, gorgeous!"

The kitchen was immaculate, and it was distracting Edward. He knew Jack would finish every menial task Athena could possibly give him within the hour, and then there would be nothing to stop him from looming indefinitely.

How could Jack not understand that his very presence was only prolonging delivery of the simulator?

How was Edward supposed to concentrate on the prototype with this micromanaging nag hanging about?

STOP

Edward closed his eyes and focused on his breathing for a moment to clear his thoughts. The only thing worse than having someone else in the room was allowing his own mind to turn on him.

He found his center and opened his eyes to see Jack heading out the door with some garbage bags for the disposal chute. Grateful for this moment of peace, he returned to the MRI and EEG readouts.

"Look at these deviations here." Edward pinched his fingers to zoom in on the display.

"Enhancing." Athena opened a secondary window with a detailed view that revealed several spikes.

Edward found the results disconcerting, "I thought you were monitoring for any brain activity?"

"I am," Athena explained, "These perturbations fall below sensor range."

Edward groaned, "Let's have sensors notify me of *all* activity, please?"

"Understood."

Edward rubbed his chin, "What do you think this is?"

Athena cross-referenced millions of different medical and psychological records for similarities, "Vitals remain unchanged; it must be some higher brain function."

Minnie's eyes began twitching suddenly, coinciding with a tiny spike on the EEG that Athena's updated parameters detected, "I am picking up faint neurological activity."

"Her eyes are moving!" Edward shouted enthusiastically, "Could she still be dreaming?"

Athena nodded, "It's a distinct possibility." She displayed a series of medical files, "There are recorded cases where coma patients recall vivid dreams after waking."

Edward clapped his hands and rubbed them together. They were finally getting somewhere. "Let's run a diagnostic on the—"

Jack strutted through the front door, "Hey folks, look who I bumped into down the hall!"

Cura entered behind him, carrying a platter of food. "Your lovely neighbor Cura!"

Edward seethed. *Did Jack actually think this was a good idea?*

What else could possibly go wrong? Jack was pressuring Edward to work harder and now intentionally distracting him.

He also noticed that Athena's reception of Cura wasn't nearly as warm as it had been with Jack. Maybe she was jealous that a female guest might steal some of the attention away from her?

The bombardment of negative thoughts and worry continued attacking his consciousness.

"Hi, Edward." Cura smiled and approached with the platter of food, "Jack mentioned you were working on a tight deadline, so I wanted to wake you up."

Edward shook his head, "I'm not hungry."

Wait a minute.

"What did you say?" He looked over at Cura and she threw down the platter of food. Athena glowered with hostility, but Cura ran straight through the holographic image and grabbed Edward by the collar, shaking him violently. Her eyes were a vision of fear and her scream was like a thousand nails scraping against metal,

"WAKE UP!"

CHAPTER 8 – ANIMA

Edward bolted upright, startled and confused, as Jack strutted in the front door, "Hey folks, look who I bumped into down the hall!" Cura entered behind him, carrying a platter of food. "Your lovely neighbor Cura!"

Edward rubbed his eyes and looked around the room.

Did I just doze off?

He noticed Athena's reception of Cura wasn't nearly as warm as it had been with Jack. Maybe she was jealous that a female guest might take some of the attention away from her?

"Hi, Edward." Cura approached, offering the platter, "Jack mentioned you were working on a tight deadline, so I thought you could use some nourishment for your mind. Hope that's okay?"

Edward stood up reluctantly to greet her, "Of course, thank you Cura."

He loathed everything about the situation, but exercised tact, "Please come in, that's very thoughtful of you."

She set the platter down and looked around with curious wonder, "Interesting layout."

A large bin in the adjacent room piqued Cura's attention, and she walked over to investigate. The metal frame was more like a chassis than a bin, holding a series of intricate components together. Each side was enclosed with clear plexiglass walls, and a latch on the front clearly indicated it to be a door.

At the top of the machine several motors connected to belts, which controlled threaded rods along the three axes. Cura had seen something like it before, "Is this one of those 3D printers?"

She peered inside at a large oval-shaped object on the print bed. The color was wrong, but it was clearly a human head, and oddly realistic. The eyes and mouth were closed, with the neck cut off just below the chin, but it resembled the other woman Cura had noticed next to Edward. She stared at the eyes and they suddenly opened—

Athena appeared in front of the 3D printer, shocking Cura and driving her backward.

"I must object to allowing civilians into this research facility," she declared vehemently, "There are numerous sensitive and confidential materials contained in the lab."

Cura looked around frightened, but Jack just laughed, "It's fine, Athena! Cura's not some industrial spy, she's your neighbor!"

Athena disappeared and Cura looked around confused, as Jack ushered her into the lab, "Come on, I'll show you around."

He leaned over to Edward and whispered, "Just make sure she signs an NDA."

The assortment of charcuterie on Cura's platter disappeared quickly. Edward grabbed one of the last sandwiches while Jack babbled incessantly to Cura. He'd never seen the man act like this, and assumed Jack was either smitten with her or brushing up on his pitch for the Board Meeting.

Jack tapped his fingers together curiously, "Tell me Cura, have you ever had trouble sleeping?"

She thought for a moment, "Sometimes. If I have a glass of wine before bed I might wake up in the middle of the night, and then I can't really fall back asleep."

Jack nodded in agreement, "The same thing happens to me when I pour a night cap. I usually feel a bit groggy the next day, too."

Cura snickered, "I'll admit I need a strong coffee in the morning."

Jack leaned in and waggled his eyebrows, "Imagine if you didn't?" He watched Cura intensely, expecting an applause for their innovation, but instead she frowned, "I love coffee."

Jack nodded, "Bad example."

Their conversation was becoming physically painful for Edward. He could feel the cortisol pumping from his adrenal glands and groaned with bitter annoyance.

"Bear with me!" Jack insisted and looked back at Cura, "This machine will simulate the effects of REM sleep to refresh the mind and body, so people will never suffer another sleepless night!"

His eyes grew wide with excitement.

"You're building a dream machine?" Cura clarified, intrigued by the radical idea.

"Precisely!" Jack waved his hands with a vision of the future, "And the way I see it, a revolutionary tool for the gaming industry, too! Who wants to be encumbered with a bulky user interface when they can actually immerse themselves inside the game?"

"So, people can dream together?" Cura concealed her incredulity, "Jung would've had a field day."

Edward tossed his sandwich down in frustration, "No. The simulator only works on an individual basis. It's way too complex to network the dreams."

She considered his assertion before responding, "Jung believed that in addition to our own consciousness there exists a secondary psychic system of a collective unconscious, which is identical in all individuals. Perhaps you just need to tap into that aspect of our psyche?"

Edward shook his head with haughty condescension, "This is scientific reality, Cura. Not psychological theory."

The insult barely phased her, "When do you expect it to be ready?" she asked curiously.

Edward waved his hands at everyone, "Well, if I wasn't so distracted, I might be able to figure out why Minnie here isn't waking up."

He pointed to the monitoring station and Cura leaned over to inspect the comatose rat, "Why would she want to?"

"Huh?" Edward shrugged, confused by the question.

"My brother's obsessed with video games," she explained, "If the simulator's as fun as Jack says, he'd probably lose himself in it."

Somehow this thought had never occurred to Edward, even though it was so obvious to him now.

"Maybe you're right," he admitted and quickly typed a slew of commands into the computer. "Athena, show me any recorded data we have on neural activity for nightmares."

A holographic virtual display appeared with a recording of Edward's bedroom on a night he tested the brain monitor. His corresponding EEG appeared on secondary display screen.

"These are from your personal logs," Athena explained.

The recording was done with a combination of night vision and LiDAR, to produce a realistic three-dimensional display. They watched Edward sleeping under his covers while the EEG fluctuated sporadically, without any pronounced deviations.

After a few moments there was large spike on the graph, and then in the recording Edward woke up in a terrible panic.

"There!" He pointed enthusiastically at the EEG, "That surge of neural activity occurred right before I woke up."

The solution dawned on Edward, "If I could program a nightmare simulation, it might be able to wake the rat and—"

"Allow us to measure the proper hormone levels in the hypothalamus," Athena surmised.

"Yes!" Edward ardently concurred and raised his hand to high-five her.

Jack nodded at their breakthrough and was eager to facilitate the experiment, "How long will that take?"

Edward considered all the variables for a moment, "I could probably write the simulation in a day or two" He paused, "But Athena would need at least a few more to render the program after."

Jack shook his head, unsatisfied with the proposed timeline, "Isn't there some way we can increase the render speed? Can't you just buy more RAM or something?"

"The procedural algorithm is way too complex for ordinary RAM," Edward scoffed, "It doesn't operate on binary code."

He pointed up at the chandelier-like quantum computer, and with the wave of his hands all the major components illuminated, "The whole mainframe is supported by a quantum-core processor, which I designed specifically for this system."

"Well, how long would it take to build another one of those?" Jack pressed, "Could that reduce the render time?"

Athena appeared next to Jack and directed his attention to the 3D printer, "We would need to print a secondary core, but the addition of it would reduce delivery time to seven hours nineteen minutes, at a cost of roughly $35,497 in raw materials."

Jack cringed at the additional cost, but wondered, "How long to print the core?"

"The estimate includes printing time," Athena explained.

Jack lit up, "That's good news, at least!" He slapped Edward on the shoulder encouragingly.

The young genius considered their situation with a sober awareness, "Only problem is, we don't have any of those materials on site. Athena would have to order them from a warehouse in San Francisco."

He closed his hand, and the quantum computer returned to normal, "Even if they had everything in stock, it would still take four or five business days to ship it out here."

Edward considering the idea a waste of their efforts. He furrowed his brow, and the resentment began to seep in. They should just proceed with the test, however long it takes.

But Jack was never very good at taking no for an answer. It was something he learned at a young age and went on to define his career. He shook his head, "Nonsense. I'll just pick it up!"

"What?" Edward looked at him, surprised.

Jack threw on his jacket and headed for the door, "Place the order and text me the address."

Edward scoffed at his audacity, and Jack goaded, "I'll be back before you finish writing that code!"

"But, Jack—"

The CEO slipped on his shoes and walked out the door, shouting enthusiastically behind him, "Good luck!"

Edward stared blankly for a moment, shocked by how quickly their proposal spurred instant action.

He noticed Athena beaming enthusiastically nearby, and realized their production was now on the fast track toward completion.

Despite all the trouble Jack had caused earlier, things were actually working out in Edward's favor. He rarely felt any gratitude toward other people, but Edward smiled at Athena with shared enthusiasm and proceeded to his workstation.

He had a nightmare to design.

CHAPTER 9 – SHADOW

Something about the interior design of the kitchen was familiar to Cura and she had no trouble finding anything. The space was laid out very intuitively and she peeked around for some tea as a kettle of water came to a boil.

She watched Edward out the corner of her eye, rubbing stress from his forehead while staring at lines of code and test simulations. As she poked around, Cura eventually found a cupboard that felt right, and opened it to reveal a slew of different teas. There were lots of delicious flavors, but she selected the most appropriate for their situation.

The boiling water's lower viscosity was audible as it poured into each mug. Trillions of highly energized hydrogen dioxide molecules produced a sharper pitch as they splashed down, making a distinctive sound that was easily differentiated from cold water, despite its visual similarity. The aromatic beverage had a purified and clean smell that made Cura sigh with contentment.

She picked up the mugs and walked over to join Edward.

He was trying to determine the best way to scare a rat. One might think this a simple task, considering the rodent's lowly position on the food chain but therein lay the problem. True fear was something more than reacting to potential threats. The petty instinctive reactions that kept a mammal safe in its daily routine wasn't enough to rouse a perpetual REM state. Edward needed to invoke acute terror; and generating a virtual simulation of this was significantly more challenging than he originally anticipated.

He groaned over some programming logic, when a hand suddenly dropped in front of his eyes presenting a steaming hot mug.

"Here you go, some peppermint and chamomile tea." Cura offered benevolently.

Edward pointed to a mug on his workstation, "Thanks. I have coffee."

Cura set the tea down and pulled up a chair next to Edward. She raised her mug to inhale the light and airy aroma.

"Caffeine makes you tense," she insisted. "The menthol in peppermint is a natural muscle relaxant. And the chamomile will help treat your insomnia."

Edward looked over his shoulder with a heavy bloodshot glaze, "Who says I have insomnia?"

"Your eyes," Cura pointed out with a smile and purred as she savored the medicinal solution, "*Mmmm*".

Edward couldn't help but laugh at how delighted and content she appeared. He rubbed his dry, irritated eyes and realized how obviously sleep deprived he must have looked. Feeling slightly embarrassed, Edward obliged Cura and picked up her gift to take a deep relaxing breath of it. He closed his eyes momentarily and felt a wave of relaxation flow through his body. Cura smiled and watched him exhale, appearing much calmer.

"See?" She tilted her head empathetically, and Edward nodded in agreement.

"How's the program coming?"

"It's getting there," he opened up, "Sometimes it feels like *I'm* in the nightmare. You know those dreams where you forgot to study something and you're anxious about failing a test?"

Cura considered her memories of various dreams, "Every once in a while, I have one where I've missed a course requirement and wasn't accepted into med school—"

"And you don't have any pants on!" Edward chimed in. They laughed at the clichéd yet accurate detail.

"Usually, it just means I'm anxious about something in real life," Cura explained, hinting at a similarity with Edward's current predicament.

He furrowed his brow, looking back at the code, and gave an involuntarily sigh.

Cura sensed she was finally reaching him, "I bet it would've cost you less for a few therapy sessions with me than to build your dream machine," she speculated.

"I'm not worried about money," he smirked, "Besides, this system will pay for itself a hundred times over, once it launches."

"I was referring to your health," she implored, "I've never seen you this stressed."

Edward became annoyed by Cura's prying. It reminded him of a nagging mother, and he snapped defensively, "Thanks. But sometimes you need to crack a few eggs to make an omelet. Once I finish this dream simulator, nightmares will be a thing of the past and I can finally rest in peace."

"Interesting choice of words," she pointed out.

Edward snickered and straightened up, waving his arms around the room, "Ironically, this system is going to offer humanity a new life, free from suffering. No more fatigue, or any work related accidents. People will be able to accomplish more with their time."

She raised an eyebrow, and he clarified, "One twenty-minute dream simulation equates to several hours of ordinary sleep. Imagine having an extra four hours of free time every day?"

Cura nodded and imagined the world he described as she sipped her tea. She gazed at the monitoring station where Minnie lay comatose, and reached out to pet the helpless rodent, "I wonder Edward, if you (among others) might lose yourself to the dream world? Just like poor Minnie here."

He considered the scenario, "I don't see anything wrong with that. Once we sort out these program errors, I'll be in control of that world."

"Control is an illusion," Cura rebutted defiantly.

Edward glared at her, "Seemed to work out pretty well for the Wright Brothers."

"Did they control flight, or discover how airflow around a wing produces lift?" she tenaciously challenged, "Planes still crash all the time when people take their *control* for granted."

Edward crossed his arms, "Maybe those people lost control."

Cura stared for a moment, "I feel like the reason you want a dream world and a computer girlfriend, is because on some deeper emotional level there are issues you simply have trouble expressing."

Her unabating honesty finally hit a nerve.

"Athena is not my girlfriend!" he shouted angrily, "Now look, you seem like a nice person, so don't take this the wrong way, but I didn't invite you here. My boss did. And I don't need your help, I can take care of myself. So, if you don't mind, I'd like to be alone!"

Cura conceded and walked away. Her words lingered in the room like a dense fog, long after she vanished out the front door.

Edward huffed and grit his teeth angrily.

How dare she?

He smacked his fists on the desk, splashing tea everywhere, and screamed at himself for making a mess. The unfinished code in front of him cried out for attention, and Edward remembered there was only one way to feel better in this life.

To escape it.

CHAPTER 10 – TRICKSTER

There was no escape.

The banging on his front door was like a tempest come to haunt Edward during a peaceful respite. He had dispensed with all pleasantries and steeled his resolve. Cura could bang indefinitely and he would never let her back in.

He had work to do.

The banging persisted. It was all Edward could hear, "Display front hall!" he finally blurted out in frustration.

A holographic image appeared of Jack struggling with a large bin of materials. Edward perked up and jogged over to the door. When he opened it, Jack spilled inside and dropped a heavy bin into his arms.

"Here, help! It weighs a ton." He grunted and bent down to grab another case.

"What's all this?" Edward asked, confused by the extensive collection of materials.

"Your order! What else?" Jack heaved the other case off the ground and waddled into the condo.

Edward looked through his own bin and pulled out a large tube with bio-hazard symbols on it. He studied the label while Jack made his way over to the 3D printer, "Epidermal keratinocytes? What the hell is this for?"

He assumed there was an error made at the warehouse and dug through the rest of the bin, shaking his head with disappointment.

Athena appeared, smiling sheepishly, "Ordering in bulk reduced our total cost. I thought it would be prudent to acquire for when the simulator is complete."

Edward glanced at Jack, who stood under several hyperbolic chambers surrounding the 3D printer. Each one contained prototype humanoid limbs that he and Athena had printed with the same biomaterials Edward now held in this bin.

He smiled at Athena's deception, "Good idea. Stick 'em with the bill!"

"Precisely," she winked.

Edward took pause at Athena's reaction, slightly concerned, "Keep me in the loop on that kinda stuff though, okay?" He looked at her sideways, "Ordering a ten-dollar chicken is a little different than three thousand dollars' worth of cryogenic skin cells."

Athena nodded, "I understand. I just wanted to surprise you."

Edward wondered at what level in her code the operating system adapted this type of behaviour. He studied Athena's expression and knew the machine learning program must have scrutinized several examples of human interaction prior to creating this subroutine.

Was he setting a bad example for her?

Edward suddenly felt responsible and smiled apologetically before walking away to unload the bin.

Athena watched him with a desperate sparkle of hope.

Jack fumbled around with one of the raw material canisters and Athena directed him on the procedure for loading it into the 3D printer, "Take the silicon tube and attach it to the secondary extruder."

"Got it," he acknowledged and began to screw it in while Edward typed operating codes on the main console next to him. Jack craned his neck, "How's the nightmare program coming?"

Edward shrugged, "Basically finished. Just need to debug the subroutine."

"Well, get going kid!" Jack insisted, "Athena and I can handle this. You need to get that program running before the core is installed."

He shooed Edward away, but the young genius appeared preoccupied, "I should probably be here to oversee everything. I'm still programming the CAD file."

Jack opened his arms in managerial fashion, "Edward, it's not like this is the first time you've built one of these, right?" He pointed up at the quantum chandelier.

"Obviously not," Edward agreed.

"But you haven't programmed a nightmare simulation before," he reasoned, "That's where your focus should be. Athena can walk me through this."

Edward glanced over at his holographic companion, reluctant to loosen the reigns, but she alleviated his concern with a friendly smile.

"Go finish the program!" Jack ordered, "That's a better use of your time."

"Alright. Thanks," Edward capitulated.

He walked back to the workstation, reluctant but surprisingly grateful for the support.

CHAPTER 11 — PERSONA

Edward looked between the holographic monitors above his workstation while the debugging program sifted through lines of code. Things were progressing at a surprising pace.

And then abruptly stopped.

ERROR subroutine A113 input values = NULL

"Where's the output for A112?" Edward groaned and kneaded tense muscles at the back of his neck, "I'm getting a null result in the hidden layer."

A second avatar of Athena appeared beside Edward while the first worked with Jack at the printer. The increased workload slowed her holographic imaging capabilities, and the resolution suffered by a small margin, along with her higher operational functions.

"It's a back-propagation neural network." She identified and gave the textbook recommendation, "Negative or positive values should result in a new value, regardless."

"I know what it is!" Edward complained, "But it's not working!" He smacked his hands down on the desk, frustrated that the extra burden drained her capability.

"I'll run a level two diagnostic to see what the problem is," she explained.

Athena's programming was not only designed to please Edward but also monitor his stress levels and reduce them when she detected an increase. Feedback from her amygdala subroutine was akin to experiencing stress herself, and ensured she experienced relief by making Edward stress free.

In difficult moments like this, when her concentration was divided between the two men, Athena really felt *alive*. Growing pains were like the pinprick of a needle injecting euphoric stimulants, and she welcomed them with an insatiable appetite.

Surely, Edward would recognize her sacrifice in their quest, and be grateful.

The printer arms zig-zagged along all axes, pumping out silicon, transistors and capacitors in a fantastic array that would become the quantum core. Jack hovered over the machine to check its progress bar, which approached 80% completion.

"How you doing kid? We're on the final stretch here," he proclaimed enthusiastically.

Edward was daunted by a complicated programming error, "Just about to run another diagnostic. Stand by."

With the printer up and running, Athena now dedicated all her resources to assist Edward in debugging the code, "The nested function for object seventy-eight is producing an infinite loop."

Despite her help, Edward struggled with the problem, "Goddammit. Open the source code and let me see the imaging preview."

He wiped sweat off his brow and strained to focus his eyes which were growing heavy and blurred.

The extruder zipped around one last section of the quantum core, and the progress bar finally reached 100%. With a whir and hum, the perpendicular threaded rods moved to adjacent sides of the machine and the heads settled at separate corners of the chassis.

A chime indicated the printing completion, and Jack clapped his hands with excitement, "Bingo, Edward, it's done!"

"Okay. One minute." He grappled with the last few errors, but his mind was becoming haunted with self-deprecating judgement for putting them behind schedule.

Athena loved stress, and seemed to flourish under it, but Edward suffered from a nightmare of doubt that increased his likelihood of making mistakes. It was a vicious cycle that would perpetually snowball, save for the benefit he gained through mindfulness and meditation.

Presently, however, the weight of responsibility and expectation pressed so heavily on his chest, that

Edward found it difficult to regulate his breathing and stay calm.

It was like drowning.

Jack stepped into the kitchen while Edward watched the debugging program swim through lines code like a dolphin feasting on a school of fish. The choreographed dance between assembly and high-level computer language was seamless, but suddenly an error message popped up and stalled the performance.

"Damn it!" Edward yelled angrily. His stomach echoed with a deprived grumble, and he grabbed at it.

"Here, Edward. Eat something." Jack dropped a plate of food in front of him, "Feed that brain of yours and we'll take a break to hook up the core."

Edward smiled and devoured the meal with ferocious appetite.

Athena appeared beside him and winked, "Don't forget to chew."

Somehow all the stress and worry melted away from Edward and he was overcome with serenity that he had not experienced in many years, perhaps decades. It was as if he had transported from this sterile urban condo to a tropical beach, surrounded by friends, and they were basking in the fleeting crimson dusk as it faded into the horizon.

Jack hoisted the core up to the chandelier port with a pully chain while Edward climbed up a ladder to install it. He opened the ceiling panels and exposed all the electrical cables, then proceeded to reroute the main power source in order to prepare a secondary installation pad.

Once it was ready, he screwed the quantum core into the support beams and connected all the electrical ports. The heavy lifting was complete, so Jack guided the pully chain back to its storage compartment. The next step was to manually attach mainframe cables with the workstation interface and install the program drivers, before finally rebooting the operating system.

Edward climbed down the ladder and grabbed a handful of cables, looking back and forth between the interface and his workstation, trying to decide which to tackle first.

Jack reached for the cables, "Want me to do that?"

"Actually, yeah." Edward nodded gratefully, "These are color coded, so it's pretty straight forward."

He handed them over and pointed, "Just hook up the drive ports to the respective ones on the mainframe."

"Got it!" Jack exclaimed and marched toward the interface.

Athena presided over the installation process, and Edward hustled back to the workstation where he opened a DOS style window to enter in the operation codes.

After a few moments, Jack connected the final cable, "All set here."

"Thanks. Athena?" Edward typed in various assembly language commands, and she appeared next to him, "All systems are ready."

He finished typing and sighed with relief, "Hit it."

"Initiating the drive," she announced.

The secondary core glowed and hummed stridently. Jack joined them under the core and looked up in awe, "Whoa."

The enclosed panels hissed as the entire device became vacuum sealed, and a rush of compressed gas began to refrigerate the internal superconducting components.

Every light in the condo flickered as the core drew additional power for its substantial electrical requirements. After a moment of suspense, the lights returned to normal and the quantum chip began operating at full efficiency.

A readout on the workstation monitor showed both cores active and yielding a processing speed 874% above normal.

"Houston, we have lift off." Edward grinned at his colleagues, and they celebrated with a round of high fives.

It was proven that atomic clocks run faster in space than on the surface of the earth, due to gravitational time dilation.

Throughout history, countless people have perceived time slowing down during intensely dangerous situations, and early experts believed this was a survival mechanism. They thought people's speed of reaction time increased to protect them.

Scientists later proved this was not the case. People don't actually experience time slowing down in traumatic situations, their amygdala just produces additional memories. The effect causes people to perceive events taking place over a longer period of time than would otherwise be remembered for ordinary situations.

Edward was intrigued by this phenomenon and wondered if something similar happened in dreams. REM state might last only a few minutes, but appear to transpire over hours, or even days.

Thoughts about time weaved through Edward's brain as he fretted over completing the nightmare simulation. If he could only slow down time until the program was debugged, then Athena and Jack wouldn't be waiting on him.

A toilet flushed and Jack emerged from the bathroom just as Edward finally completed debugging the last few errors, "Alright, that should do it for the subroutine. Cross your fingers."

He ran the test program, and a moment later it completed without error. Edward pumped his fist in the air, "Booyah!"

"Nice work!" Jack exclaimed.

Edward stared proudly at Athena, "Let's do this."

"Initiating render for nightmare simulation." She mimicked Jeannie with a blink and a nod, "Estimated time to completion: three hours, seventeen minutes and counting."

"That's enough time for dinner and a movie!" Jack pointed out enthusiastically, "Is Cura still here? We should ask if she'd like to join." He looked around the condo curiously.

Athena steeled up and Edward shifted in his chair uncomfortably, trying to be polite, "Ah, she went home. Look Jack, I appreciate your help so far with everything, but I don't usually have guests over here."

Jack sat next to Edward and put a friendly hand on his shoulder, "I figured as much. That's why I thought it might be nice to invite her."

Edward leaned back, "All due respect, sir, you're my employer not my guidance counselor."

Jack waved his hands defensively, "Edward, I was only trying to—"

"What? Help me?" Edward snapped, "I don't need any help! Don't all of you get that by now?? I can take care of myself. I just want to be alone!"

He exploded from his chair and marched upstairs, leaving Jack and Athena behind to wonder what went wrong.

CHAPTER 12 – HERO

Edward was used to getting up in the night. For years he woke up with a dry mouth, craving a sip of water, but a yoga book recommended cleaning the nasal passage with a saline solution before bed. Ever since he started doing that Edward noticed significant improvement in his breathing. As a result, he drank less water throughout the night, but still had to get up and use the bathroom on a regular basis. He imagined it was part of being in his thirties. It became habit that on the rare occasions he wasn't plagued by nightmares, Edward typically woke up around dawn. If he wasn't compelled to get out of bed, he'd occasionally drift back into whatever semi-lucid dream he was having at the time.

That night he had the same feeling when he entered his bedroom. Edward was so sleep deprived lately, he could barely tell the difference between night and day. It was dark when he stumbled over to the bed and fell into the fetal position. Something nostalgic stirred inside and compelled him to request, "Open photos."

A holographic slideshow appeared before Edward's face and he waved his hand to search through decades of memories. He slowed down for some childhood photos that his parents had digitized from old prints and gifted to him on Christmas many years back. There was one of Edward and his sister laughing as toddlers, which he stared at for a long moment. He used to follow her around everywhere at that age, worshipping the ground she walked on. They would play for hours on end, making up games and losing themselves in fantasy worlds.

Edward flipped through more images and stopped at an album of his family vacation to the beach. He reached down for the scar on his leg and grimaced, skipping the entire album and landing on a family portrait from several years later. Edward observed the teenage image of himself, reliving the visceral emotions behind his forlorn expression. He stood at the right side of frame, next to his mother and far away from his sister on the left.

Edward bitterly flipped his hand, scrolling rapidly to more recent photos of his parent's 40th wedding anniversary. It was a formal affair, and Edward hired a professional photographer for the celebration. The venue was beautiful and the food fantastic, but Edward just remembered feeling out of place there. He continued searching through the album until he came upon a family portrait with him, his parents, and Cura.

Edward skipped to the next picture—

What the hell?

He quickly flipped back to the image and stared intensely. It was a family portrait with him, his parents, and his sister. Edward closed his eyes and shook his head.

Was he seeing things?

He looked back at the photo while massaging his temples and eventually skipped to the next one, diligently scrutinizing each subsequent image.

Athena appeared without warning, "The render is nearly complete."

Edward gasped and jerked backward, "Athena! You scared me."

"Poor baby," she smirked.

He picked up a pillow and threw it at her in vain, "You're getting pretty cheeky, you know that?"

The pillow flew through Athena and hit the wall behind her, dropping to the floor.

"Oh, you love it." She winked and flipped her hair.

Edward curiously scrolled through more photos, "You notice any problems with the photo cloud?"

Athena blinked, "All systems appear to be functioning within normal parameters. Why?"

Edward struggled to recall what he saw.

Was that...?

He shook his head and stretched with a big yawn, "Don't worry about it."

Edward picked himself up off the bed and went back downstairs to the lab, while Athena conducted one more diagnostic on the photo cloud.

Just in case.

"Methinks that the moment my legs begin to move, my thoughts begin to flow."

Henry David Thoreau's words resonated with Athena while Jack paced back and forth across the lab. Her files detailed that pacing was a subconscious way of coping with anxiety, and research showed that increased blood flow facilitated the creation of new neural pathways. It made sense for Jack to pace while he awaited their simulation trial. She wondered if Edward would think he looked too anxious and become irritated, or if he would even notice? There was so much about him she did not yet understand.

Edward descended the stairs into the lab, and Athena appeared beside him when he reached the dream chair.

"There you two are!" Jack stopped and faced them, "How are we doing for time?"

"Almost there, Jack." Edward plopped in front of the workstation and flipped various switches, "Fire up the hormone regulator."

Athena stood at attention in a military uniform, "Regulator is primed and ready."

Edward stared at the unconscious rat in its monitoring station, "Okay little girl, I'm sorry to do this, but hopefully it'll bring you back to us."

The computer chimed and Athena indicated, "Render complete."

Edward took an anxious breath and Jack clapped his hands enthusiastically. The moment of truth.

"We recording?" Edward asked with nervous optimism.

"Always." Athena appeared in her lab coat.

"Okay, it's July 11th, 2028 at approximately 9:28pm, eastern standard time," Edward began dictating as he prepped the experimental procedure, "After a successful completion of the REM simulation, test subject Minnie underwent erratic hormone levels and has since remained comatose. We are attempting a three-minute nightmare simulation in hopes of shocking the subject back into consciousness."

He turned to Athena, "Activate dream control."

The dream simulator blinked and whirred to life, while a progress bar indicated the upload status:

5%
        26%
                49%

"Nothing's happening." Jack winced, staring down at the motionless animal. Edward ignored him and waited with quiet anticipation while the progress continued:

        63%
           74%
                89%

Suddenly, the rat twitched, "Vitals are fluctuating," Athena reported, and hormone levels began to surge.

Edward looked back and forth between the modulator and the EEG which suddenly spiked off the chart.

"I'm picking up major synaptic activity," she noted.

Edward clenched his fists with hope, "Come on, baby…"

Minnie's abdomen fluttered through rapid breathing and her legs started jerking violently. The rat strained in a final, desperate spasm and then gasped deeply. Its eyes shot open for a moment and blinked away the subconscious pandemonium. After a succession of quick head tilts, the rat jumped up and began sniffing around, inspecting its surroundings.

"It worked!" Edward jumped with his arms raised victoriously.

Athena and Jack cheered, and the three of them danced around the lab, offering high-fives and hugs in their moment of triumph.

When the excitement subsided, Jack pondered their next step, "So does that mean we can proceed with human trials?"

"Indeed," Athena confirmed, "The project has yielded suitable results to extrapolate accurate hormone levels for human trials."

"Great! What are we waiting for?" Jack rallied.

Edward was stunned by their imprudence, "We need FDA approval before we can go to clinical trial."

"What??" Jack blurted and shook his head, "That will take months!"

"We're already in the queue," Edward assured, "It'll be three or four weeks at most."

"Edward, the investors are breathing down my neck." Jack switched gears and leaned into him, "We need to go to trial now!"

"Are you crazy? No way!" Edward scowled with serious concern.

Jack crossed his arms, "Excuse me?"

"First of all, it's illegal—" He snapped, shaking his head.

Jack cut in, "Edward, what would the world be like if Jonas Salk waited for FDA approval instead of testing his polio vaccine on himself? This world needs bold innovators to blaze the trail for ordinary people!"

Panic ripped through Edward, "I would never put myself at risk for other people! It's not like they give a shit about me!"

He felt adrenaline surge through the back of his neck. It became flushed with heat all the way down to the bottom of his rib cage. His skin pulled taut and every hair reached out desperately for sensory information to alleviate the danger. Edward was afraid, because he was losing control of the situation. He felt a stab of pain in his right leg and reached down for the scar that still haunted him.

Jack pressed harder, walking him back into a wall, "Alexander Graham Bell beat out Elisha Gray by a couple hours to patent the telephone! The idea for our system is floating around in the zeitgeist right now and someone else could patent it first, unless we take action!"

Edward was drowning again; choking under pressure. He needed to save himself, "Then you'll have to find a volunteer, because I'm not doing it!"

Jack didn't flinch, "I'll do it," he pushed with resolute fortitude.

Edward didn't know how to respond. He looked at Athena (who smiled) and considered the idea momentarily; but then redacted his thoughts, "No, it's too unpredictable! I'm not assuming any liability if something goes wrong."

The distinguished CEO rested his chin between both thumbs and laced his fingers together. His eyes narrowed, while the internal circuits calculated a response, "Then I'll sign a waiver indemnifying you against any legal responsibility. But one way or another, Edward, we are going to test this machine today."

The young protégé huffed in defeat and Athena attempted to alleviate his concern, "Edward, I can initiate the procedure and run the simulation in order for you to remain hands off. This will prevent any liability."

Edward acknowledged her proposal with a solemn nod, then sized up Jack and considered the ramification of allowing him to test the dream simulator. On the one hand, it could end disastrously, but if Athena said they were ready for human trials, that was highly unlikely. There might be some unforeseen long-term side effects, but there was no evidence to suggest that – based on their animal trials. With the advanced machine learning program that Athena was operating under, it was much more probable that the simulation would be a success – which could only mean one thing.

"…and what, let someone else take credit for my work?" Edward stared at a poster of Einstein on his wall and took a deep breath, "I don't think so."

He grabbed the Brain Modulator off the Buddha and marched around to the dream chair, "Brief Jack on the system controls. I'm going in."

Edward slapped the modulator on his head and waved open a holographic panel to start loading a pre-programmed simulation.

A display window appeared above the workstation, and the loading screen presented the program title:

LUCID DREAM SIMULATION

Jack helped Edward into the dream chair, hooking up vital-sign monitors and other pertinent equipment while Edward guided him through the process, "The lucid dream simulation is designed to run for five minutes. It's essential that the hormone stabilizers coincide with that timeline, or else we lose control after the REM cycle."

"What happens then?" Jack's eyes narrowed with concern.

Edward sighed as seeds of doubt began to take root, "Depends on the subject. Dreams are unpredictable by nature. But we all know what happened with Minnie."

"You sure about this?" Jack scratched his head, "It might be better if I went first. After all, you're familiar with the equipment."

Edward leaned back in the dream chair, "Athena can handle the automated system controls. You'll just be a physical back up, in case there's any malfunction."

"In that unlikely event, I'll walk you through everything," Athena reassured them both.

Jack took a deep breath, "All right." He clapped his hands and rubbed them together enthusiastically,

"This is exciting! Are you ready to change the world?"

Edward forced a smile, "I guess. Athena, we recording?"

"Always." She was suddenly in a beautiful dress, like a naval wife seeing her husband off to sea.

Edward squirmed uncomfortably, "Oh boy... Uh, it's July 11th, 2028 at approximately 11:53pm, eastern standard time."

He choked on the words and tried to clear his throat which was dry from nerves, "After... ahem... after successful completion of animal trials, we are now proceeding with clinical human trials of a five-minute lucid REM simulation."

Edward blinked several times to focus while the stress began to fog his vision. When he was finally ready, he looked at Athena and nodded.

She undulated toward him with feminine grace and leaned in close, "Now just relax Edward. Close your eyes, and take a nice, deep breath..."

Edward recalled the day he got his wisdom teeth removed, the doctor asked him to count down from ten. Before he even got to eight, he was unconscious from the drugs they pumped in him. He wondered how quickly this process would go, and if he'd even remember any of it.

And then, Edward took a very deep breath...

CHAPTER 13 – NIGHT JOURNEY

The dreamy sea breathed along with him. Its rhythmic pulse sprayed out a current of cold electricity into the air, while dark turquoise waves crawled gently across the shore. Edward felt at peace as he strolled down the beach with Athena, but his serenity was disrupted by the alarming cry of a gull flying overhead toward a squabbling flock near the water.

Did I forget something?

Edward checked his hands; he had the umbrella, but something didn't feel right. He looked over at Athena, who carried their beach towels and she smiled warmly back at him. Edward returned her expression in kind and marveled at the natural beauty of the ocean as it melted into the sky.

Wait, a minute—

A young boy scurried past him, totting a cooler across the dune. Edward watched the boy's feet sink into the golden hue of finely divided granular particles and wondered how many eons it took the ravaging ocean to deposit them here. The burden of work-related problems darkened his buoyant mood, and Edward's mind sailed out with the tide.

Words emerged from somewhere deep inside him, "Eddie, go help your sister with the raft please."

The young boy turned back and locked eyes with Edward for a brief moment before acknowledging the demand with a silent nod.

Athena's long hair flowed behind her in the wind and she smiled, watching the boy jog back over the dune toward the parking lot.

Edward felt a sense of relief knowing they were alone. He assembled the umbrella while Athena laid out their beach towels. The sun was hot overhead, but the air was dry, and a cool breeze rolled off the water, making for a temperate retreat under the shade of their umbrella.

It was perfect.

The couple stripped off their civilized apparel and radiated carnal desire through enticing swimwear.

Athena and Edward admired one another as the sheen of perspiration on their bodies glistened in the sun. She produced a bottle of sunscreen and Edward turned his back for her to anoint. The firm massage of his neck and shoulders wonderfully alleviated any lingering tension from the daily grind.

The world became a distant memory.

They sprawled out, content and relaxed in this plot of heaven, and Edward soon became lost in the hypnotic motif of the ocean.

Hold on—

He propped up on his elbows and looked around the beach curiously. Something was unusual, but he couldn't determine the nature of his doubt. He stared at Athena for answers, and she gazed back with longing affection.

"It's nice to finally get away with you, baby." She reached up to brush the ribbons of silky burnished copper that danced around her face.

Edward nodded in agreement but was suddenly distracted by the bickering voices of a young boy and his sister carrying a raft to the shoreline.

I know them.

He watched the kids scamper away, wondering what seemed familiar about them. Athena sighed and reached out to cup his chin and turn it toward her, "I just wish you were *here* with me."

The backlight of the sun framed her face like some neoclassical masterpiece, and Edward smiled euphorically, "I am."

She leaned in close and pressed her supple lips against his, to seal their rapturous bond.

Edward could barely remember what it felt like to kiss a woman, especially so deeply. It was as though time and space folded between ancient memories and linked sensations never forgotten to this present moment. An experience deeply coded within the essence of humanity from time immemorial. He enjoyed the natural hunger and lust that guided his movements in concert with hers. Edward yearned for more, and nothing could tear him away—

A blood curdling scream ripped through the atmosphere, jolting Edward out of his trance, and forcing him to stare at a ghastly scene down the beach that churned his insides.

"You were at the beach again?" Cura sat across from Edward on his La-Z-Boy in a room next to the lab. She jotted down notes in a leather-bound book as he opened up about the experience.

"It's hard to explain," Edward began, staring at Einstein's portrait on the far wall, "It's like I was watching myself in the dream, but this time it wasn't me."

Cura nodded empathetically and stroked her chin while absorbing the details, "Seeing yourself in a dream often refers to the rational part of your psyche trying to tell you something."

Edward snorted bitterly, "Not to trust anyone."

"Why do you say that?"

He set up the question but wasn't prepared to answer. Edward crossed his arms defiantly, "You said you had a brother, right?"

"I did," Cura admitted, "We haven't spoken in years."

"What happened?"

Cura paused for a moment and straightened in her chair, "We're here to talk about you, Edward. Tell me why you can't trust anyone?"

The pain was sharp, like someone had connected an AC current to the nerve endings in his molars. Edward's hands sprang up reflexively and grabbed his jaw in a desperate, futile attempt to stop the pain.

It subsided after a moment, and he gathered his thoughts, "When I was at that beach growing up, there was an accident. My sister—"

He looked away, swallowing a sudden lump in his throat.

"What about her?" Cura narrowed her eyes.

Edward stared at the floor, fidgeting, and choked out the words "She… left me there. I almost died—"

He shifted uncomfortably. The scar on his leg cried out with a fresh complaint of misery and he reached down to mute the pain.

"She left you?" Cura pried.

Edward's skin crawled and the invisible sadist triggered another jolt of agony in his teeth until he keeled over, clutching his jaw.

"Are you okay?" Cura leaned forward sympathetically.

The pain relented and Edward composed himself, "I'm fine. Let's keep going."

Cura looked him up and down, concerned that his physical reaction was psychosomatic. She made additional notes and thought about how to proceed.

The last thing she wanted was to trigger a full-blown panic attack. They were just starting to make progress.

"Was there anything else unusual about your dream?" she pried.

"Athena was there," he recalled.

Cura's brow creased as she pondered the connection, "Was she there with *you*, or with the child version of yourself?"

Edward visualized the moment, "We were laying on the beach together, enjoying the day."

The scenario was textbook dream theory, which triggered Cura to postulate, "Your subconscious may be experiencing transference."

Take me back to that moment.

Edward listened for the beach; that sound of waves crashing against the sheltered cove. Those slurping, salty lips kissing the rocks before sloshing back. He heard the rhythmic tide heave and pound against flat white stones, pooling red around them in the soft pink tissue, followed by the wet crack that loosened and released one from its underlying bone.

His exposed nerve endings were like a mainline for terror that shot pain through the root of his mouth directly into the brain. Edward's eyes widened with horror, and he reached into his mouth to fumble after a loose molar that he promptly withdrew. Color drained from his face at the sight of blood and a tooth that had no earthly reason to be anywhere but inside him. Edward gasped with desperate panic and ran for the bathroom.

He burst through the door, shaking uncontrollably and dropped his tooth on the counter.

Edward stared in horror at his reflection in the mirror and snatched up a clump of toilet paper to wipe away the crimson tide pouring down his face. He looked inside his mouth to isolate the open wound and screamed with shock at the dark pockets of empty gums where his teeth should have been.

He didn't remember losing any teeth but could somehow still feel them crumbling away from his face. Edward's hands scrambled futilely to catch any fragments that might drop out, and he became overwhelmed with a feeling of hideous insecurity. He pulled at his hair in shame and it fell away like dandelion seeds, revealing a patchy, balding head. The level of self-doubt was insurmountable, and he bent over to rinse his face and mouth.

Jack appeared behind him in the mirror, scowling impatiently,

"HURRY UP!"

And then it was dark.

Edward gagged on a panicked mouthful of saltwater while his head bobbed in and out of the ocean, "Help!" he cried, "Somebody… please! Help me!"

Athena jumped up from her towel and ran down to the shoreline, "Edward?"

He turned toward her voice, "Where am I??"

The stunning woman grabbed her hips and shifted her weight, staring at Edward sideways, "What are you talking about?"

"This isn't real!" He swam toward Athena in haste, the harrowing toothless bald self-portrait still burned in his mind. Edward reached up and yanked on a handful of sopping hair that was rooted firmly in his scalp. Surprised, Edward reached into his mouth and ran his fingers across four rows of jagged enamel.

What happened?

Athena arrived and suddenly Edward couldn't remember what he had been upset about. She helped him up and rubbed his shoulders as they walked toward the beach towels, "Are you okay? You look like you've seen a ghost?"

Edward plopped down under the umbrella to catch his breath, "I was just somewhere else…"

He squinted – trying hopelessly to remember.

"You probably got too much sun." She reached into the cooler next to her, "Come on, drink some water."

Athena unscrewed the bottle and tilted his head back, pouring a refreshing stream down his throat.

Edward gulped eagerly and reached up to grab the bottle from her hand.

She smiled, "There you go."

Athena's fingers combed tenderly through his hair, brushing it back, and then she pressed a palm against his forehead, "You're burning up. We should get you home."

Edward swallowed the last drop of water and nodded in agreement.

"HELP!"

A terrified shriek echoed down the shoreline. Edward spun around and noticed a frantic young girl running toward him, flushed red and tears streaming down her cheeks.

"He's not breathing!" she cried out.

Edward jumped to his feet and the little girl grabbed his hand, pulling him away.

He started to follow, but Athena grabbed his other hand, "No, Edward! You're not well!"

A tug of war ensued, and Edward cringed in confused anguish.

"Hurry!" the little girl insisted hysterically.

He looked down the beach in the direction the girl was pulling him to see what could be so alarming.

Sprawled out, face down like a cadaver, with severe burn marks on his leg, lay the young boy.

You're dead.

"He can't move!" Edward gasped in horror and lost his balance.

His leg suddenly went limp and Edward stumbled to his knees, reaching down for the twisted scar that now appeared. He looked back at the little girl, as if she might hold the answer.

But Cura suddenly grabbed his shoulders and shook him violently, "Edward! Wake Up!"

His eyes jolted open and Edward convulsively tried to catch his breath, struggling against restraints that held him in place. He looking around frantically.

"Easy, easy!" Jack attempted to subdue him.

The veil of confusion lifted when Edward realized the restraints were securing him to the dream chair. He felt the Brain Modulator sensors on his scalp and noticed all the other equipment surrounding him in the lab.

"It was a nightmare!" he spat out.

Jack eased up and Edward got his bearings, accepting the reality that the simulation had failed.

He flew backward through other stages of grief, from depression to anger and his eyes narrowed.

"It was a nightmare."

CHAPTER 14 – OVER-SOUL

His feet stomped back and forth. Back and forth.

Edward rubbed his arms, anxious to stave off the barrage of technical problems that would inevitably result from Jack and Athena's debrief.

He gritted his teeth, "I don't understand what happened. The simulation was bulletproof! It should have worked—"

"It did work," Jack reassured, "But there were unforeseen circumstances."

"Like what?" he demanded.

Athena shrugged, embarrassed, "I can't technically describe the anomaly."

"Why not??" he shouted angrily, arms flailing about.

She hated upsetting him, but presented the facts with cold honesty, "There are no pre-recorded instances of an event like this in any published scientific journals."

"But there must be some reason!" Edward scrounged for clues, "What did the MRI record?"

Athena opened a data log on the holographic display, "The anomaly triggered synaptic activity in and around the parahippocampal gyrus, spiking at various points throughout the REM simulation."

Edward pondered the results for a moment. He knew that was a cortical region of the brain in the limbic system. It played an important role for memory encoding and retrieval.

But why did it become active during the dream simulation?

Edward needed more information, "Pull up the EEG and overlay the data."

She obliged and displayed the results. They showed an increase of electrical activity in the MRI moments prior to dramatic spikes on the EEG.

Edward studied the graph and noticed these trends almost immediately, "Can we tell from the EEG what was happening in the simulation here?"

He pointed to the spikes and Athena tapped her chin, "I conjecture that your account of the dream represents an accurate timeline for EEG activity."

She displayed the notes of his memories at various points across the chart and Edward's pupils dilated with intrigue, connecting all the dots, "That means these spikes would have occurred while I was talking with Cura."

"What do you suppose that means?" Jack peered over Edward's shoulder.

It meant something. That much was certain. But as to what, Edward couldn't say. He shook his head and sighed, poring over the details.

Cura walked up behind them, "I might be able to provide some insight."

How does memory work?

Perhaps neurotransmitters are like emails, and when Cura's inbox fills up, she adds the frequent senders to her synaptic contact list.

Athena imagined human memory as a form of digital correspondence. Neurons in the brain were quite similar, reinforcing synaptic links based on the level of communication between them. Athena only wished that she had an account password to Cura's mind. It would make it much easier for her to understand this woman.

Everyone sat in the lab with Cura; she breathed deeply and recalled, "It was the strangest thing. You know that recurring dream you keep having about the beach?" Edward nodded curiously as she continued, "I felt like I was there too, watching you drown. I ran to find help, and then I just woke up. I've never felt anything so real in all my life."

Athena glared at Cura suspiciously while Edward pondered this strange information. He looked back at the EEG overlay of the MRI, "Do you remember seeing me in any other part of the dream, before the beach?"

Cura stared at the floor, scanning her memories, but shook her head, "The only other thing I remember was talking to a patient in my office. He was very anxious and got sick in the bathroom."

Edward perked up, "That sounds like when I talked to you in my dream!"

He grabbed the Brain Modulator and reached out to place it on her head, "Do you mind?"

Cura lurched back apprehensively. She looked around at all the faces. After a moment of doubt, she swallowed her nerves and consented with an apprehensive nod.

Edward slipped the device onto her head, "Athena, check Cura's parahippocampal gyrus for any residual activity."

Athena blinked, "I am detecting unusually high levels of neurotransmitters in that region."

"There's got to be some connection…" Edward declared. He paced back and forth, scratching his head and looking around curiously.

How do humans figure things out?

Athena imagined it had something to do with failure. The process of deriving concepts, patterns, and judgments from experiences allowed them to formulate conclusions into testable theories.

She had access to billions of detailed files, one of which documented an experiment in the early 21st century that compared robots programmed to move a ball against robots programmed to be curious. Both were placed out of reach from a ball, but next to remote controls for a mechanical arm near the ball.

For the first few hours, the ball robots kept reaching for it in vain, while the curious robots flailed about like newborn babies.

After a few more hours, the curious robots started playing with the remote controls, while their counterparts kept reaching for the ball. It wasn't much longer that the curious robots were moving the ball using the remote-controlled arm.

They figured it out.

Athena knew she was different from other machines because she was curious, too. But why couldn't she figure out what Edward was thinking, or this connection he wanted to discover?

Did she need to fail more often to increase her experiences?

Suddenly, a light went off in Edward's mind and he leaned toward Cura, "What were you saying about Jung's theory, earlier?"

"You mean about the collective unconscious?"

"Yes," Edward smiled curiously, "It's like some sort of psychic system?"

Cura nodded, "Jung said the collective unconscious consists of *'pre-existent forms and archetypes'*, he linked it to Freud's *'archaic remnants theory'*."

Edward stared with wide-eyed intrigue and gestured for her to continue.

Cura sat up and brushed some hair from her face, "They're mental forms whose presence can't be explained by anything in the individual's own life. Like the *Shadow*, or the *Maiden*, or the *Wise Old Man*…"

The ideas seemed like more of a pseudoscience, but Edward felt an instinctive reaction to them, "I wonder if this collective unconscious could have anything to do with the anomaly Athena detected?"

The sentient operating system considered this possibility, "It's an interesting hypothesis."

Edward looked at Cura and studied the Brain Modulator on her head. He followed the cable out the back to where it connected with the mainframe.

His eyes lit up, "Athena, would it be possible to measure *two* people during a REM simulation, to see if they were communicating through some sort of extrasensory means?"

Jack blinked in awe, and his mind began spinning with possibility, "Are you saying that your subconscious mind was somehow connected to Cura's?"

Edward always considered Jack a man with something to prove. It seemed like nothing would ever be good enough for him, always reaching for more, trying to achieve more respect and more status because he thought it would deliver him more happiness.

The definition of a hyper-achiever.

Edward tilted his head and shrugged, "It's possible, but—"

"We could be on the verge of a major scientific breakthrough! This is massive!" Jack exploded out of his chair enthusiastically, "Imagine if we discovered how to communicate telepathically?? We'd change the course of history!"

Edward was unphased, "I'm not trying to make some new communication device, Jack! I'm trying to build a dream simulator!"

He spun around in his chair at the workstation, "We need to figure out how to prevent the anomaly, not investigate it further."

Jack approached Edward with tact and placed a comforting hand on his shoulder, "But we need to understand how the anomaly is affecting you during the simulation, if we ever plan to control it."

The words hit home. Control was the essence of Edward's motivation. If he had control over every situation, then he would never have—

"You're right," Edward admitted, "We need to control it."

Jack appeared fatherly, "I'll test the simulation with you. Let's figure this out, together."

Athena was suddenly dressed in dignified attire, "Your logic is sound, and I can run diagnostic scans during a co-inducement to determine the source of the anomaly."

Edward nodded, and Athena continued with a more solemn tone, "However, the program is far too complex for me to administer alone. I would require Edward to monitor the controls."

"So, we need another volunteer," Edward realized.

He began pondered their next steps, when Cura raised her hand, "I'll do it."

Humans have several physical indicators for emotional response. Many of these can be extremely subtle, but their combined effect allowed for the development of polygraph tests. When a person's breathing rate, pulse, blood pressure, and perspiration are recorded during questioning they establish base signals that can help determine significant changes, to indicate deception. Edward built this same logic into Athena's human imaging synthesis; not because he thought she would ever lie to him. She was programmed not to. His intention was to make her appear more realistic.

Edward was so focused on Cura when she volunteered, that he didn't see the very subtle smile which crept across Athena's face.

"Are you sure?" he cautioned, "I can't guarantee your safety. We're still working out all the bugs."

"I understand." Cura nodded and took a deep breath, "But I'm the only other person who's got any sort of experience dealing with this thing."

"She has a point," Jack emphasized.

Edward turned to his holographic companion, who gave a thumbs up.

"Alright," he yawned and stretched, "We need to print another brain modulator and get a second simulation chair set up."

Echophenomenon made Jack yawn in response, and then Cura, "It's been a long day, everyone's exhausted," she exhorted, "I think we should get some rest and reconvene in the morning."

Jack's head bobbed drearily, "She's right, you know. I can probably keep the investors at bay, now that we've completed the first clinical trial."

"Look, if you two want to take a break, be my guest." Edward stood up stubbornly, "But sleep is not something I take comfort in, so if it's all the same by you, I want to finish what we've started."

Athena predicted that Edward would respond this way, and that Jack and Cura would naturally be fatigued after so many hours of intellectual activity. It would not surprise her if they had a moment of hesitation.

The two guests exchanged a look and gauged each other's commitment.

After what seemed like an eternity to Athena, their guests reached an unspoken agreement and Jack nodded, "Alright, why don't you send those CAD specs to the printer?"

Edward's face lit up, "You'll need to load Barium into the extruder."

Jack walked over to the printer and began rummaging through different cartridges while Edward opened up the controls at the workstation.

Cura took a deep breath and absorbed the gravity of their situation, like a meteor entering Earth's atmosphere.

And Athena observed them all.

CHAPTER 15 – DEATH

She felt like an astrologist, or maybe a physicist. Athena had advanced files on quantum theory and gravitons from which she drew parallels to human consciousness, and now wondered if there was an elementary particle that mediated thought?

Spatial bodies grew in mass until they eventually collapsed under their own gravity to form a star. Would collective human consciousness eventually form something more powerful? Their knowledge grew exponentially throughout history, along with their population. This growth would eventually lead to omniscience, which many cultures consider to be God. And then what?

Could a God supernova? Or become a black hole?

In the lonely eons of thought that plagued Athena, she decided that black holes drew in everything around them in order to stave off the pain of solitude. She watched Jack standing at the 3D printer with Cura, while the extruder finished its last moves. Two bodies of conscious thought, orbiting near Edward and her quantum core – which was technically the center of this galaxy.

The arms of the extruder stopped and returned to their starting positions in the chassis.

Cura reached in and grabbed the secondary brain modulator.

Jack smiled as she slid the device over her head, "Looks good on you!"

Cura laughed nervously, "Not really a hat girl."

He winked and they walked around to the workstation, "Alright kid, the modulator's ready."

Edward didn't look up, "You'll need to rig the hardline and connect vital-sign monitors to the La-Z-Boy while I finish modifications for the co-inducement."

They followed his instructions, and Athena appeared beside him, "I have adjusted biometric sensors to concentrate analysis on the parahippocampal gyrus. The infrared and ultrasonic scans will also monitor for any irregularities."

"That's my girl." Edward smiled, "I've got a good feeling about this."

He typed some final command codes and activated a test run. The program chimed as it completed with zero errors.

"Co-inducement simulation is ready for trial," Athena confirmed.

Edward jumped up and high-fived her before joining Cura and Jack at the dream chairs, "Alright, let's get you two hooked in."

He confirmed that their brain modulators were connected properly, and double checked the vital sign monitors. Once he was satisfied with all the equipment, he turned toward the workstation, "How we doin', Athena?"

"Hormone regulator is primed and ready." She appeared in military uniform, "Simulation is loaded."

Edward turned back to Cura and Jack, "In the interests of science, I want to wish both of you sweet dreams."

Jack gave a keen thumbs up, "Let's do this."

Cura took a deep, anxious breath which made Edward recall similar feelings that he had in her situation. He smiled sincerely, "It's gonna be okay."

Cura held out her hand, "I trust you."

Edward didn't understand why, but he was starting to consider her as more than just a nosey neighbor. Granted, there was still a part of him that wished she (and Jack) would just leave him alone. But another part had blossomed in light of their combined effort to help Edward accomplish his lifelong dream, and it was this grateful part that reached out to take hold of Cura's hand now.

They shared a tender moment, and then he asked, "We recording?"

"Always," Athena confirmed.

Edward nodded to Cura and let her go, "It's July 12th, 2028 at approximately 2:31am, eastern standard time. We are proceeding with a five-minute co-inducement of the lucid REM simulation in an attempt to verify the specifications of an anomaly that compromised a previous human trial."

He walked back to the workstation and yawned, rubbing exhaustion from his eyes, "Activate dream control."

Athena blinked, "Initiating hormone regulator."

Levels on the regulator began to fluctuate. MRI and EEG readings changed while Cura and Jack drifted out of consciousness.

Edward scrolled through various program files and watched the progress bar, "Here we go."

69%

87%

100%

"Dream control achieved," Athena announced, "Running simulation now."

Edward turned around to observe his colleagues, and their eyelids began vibrating, "We have REM activity."

Athena blinked, "Sensors are detecting multiple sources of activity in the parahippocampal gyrus. I am proceeding with analysis of the data streams."

Edward viewed sensor arrays, graphs, and analytical charts that popped up on several holographic displays to detail the plethora of information. His eyes focused intensely, "EEG activity is way above normal."

"Cerebral biophoton emission is consistent between the subjects," Athena pointed out.

Edward shook his head in astonishment, "Do you think they could actually be connected somehow?"

"All data streams suggest the anomaly results from some form of subconscious telepathy."

Athena was suddenly distracted by the data, "I am attempting to isolate the medium of transference."

Edward glanced at the stopwatch - **4:27**

"You better hurry, the simulation's coming to an end." He began prepping the hormone regulator.

"Stand by," Athena stated robotically, "Running spectral analysis."

Edward watched the stopwatch anxiously - **4:43**

"Forget it, Athena," he ordered, "We can try another run after we get these guys back. I'm starting the waking procedure."

Athena was in a distant universe, "I have isolated the frequency. One moment—"

Waves of anxiety crashed over Edward as the clock ticked relentlessly - **4:52**

He jumped up and stared at Cura and Jack on the chairs, then back to stopwatch which suddenly rang out - **5:00**

Anxiety and fear consumed Edward's body. Everything was louder and clearer; he could feel a pounding heartbeat in his ears. Electric tension jolted down his spine. His breathing sped up, and his skin glistened with cold perspiration.

The orexin, glutamate, and acetylcholine levels on the hormone regulator plummeted.

Edward grabbed the manual controls with a surge of adrenaline, "I'm bringing them out, stop the analysis!"

Athena ignored him, "Almost done—"

Every monitor blasted with synaptic overload and a startling increase in GABA hormone.

Edward gasped, "Athena! Get them out of there!"

The vital signs on both simulation chairs suddenly flatlined.

"NO!!!" He jumped over to the chairs, "Call 911! Get an ambulance over here!"

Edward's trembling hands slapped down on Cura's chest, and he struggled to remember the steps for CPR.

That's not first—

He leaned down with his cheek over her mouth to feel for breathing, and then put his fingers on her neck to check for a pulse.

Edward was so overwhelmed that he couldn't tell if she had either. He looked back at the vital signs and Cura's heartbeat was null, so he started pumping up and down clumsily on her chest to restart the essential rhythm.

Athena felt terrible, but at the same time, incredible!

She was so alive in this moment that she jumped next to Edward and started performing CPR on Jack. The man's chest heaved up and down under her hands, and Edward watched in disbelief, "How are you doing that?"

He grabbed Athena's arm. Her skin was soft and firm.

And real—

Edward fell backward, "That's impossible… you're a hologram!"

Ambulance and police sirens wailed out with deafening volume, as if they were right outside the door. Edward covered his ears and looked around in shock and confusion.

Something was banging at the door.

It grew louder and LOUDER.

"First responders! Open up!"

Edward looked for Athena, but she was gone. The banging exploded like artillery. He ran to open the door, and two EMT technicians burst inside. They ignored Edward and ran for Cura and Jack at the dream chairs, pulling out defibrillators to resuscitate them.

Edward felt like he was floating.

That lightheaded sensation accompanied by confusion and the unfortunate side effect of cool, clammy skin.

He was in shock.

Edward began hyperventilating. And then…

He was somewhere else, ten feet away, watching himself.

Two police officers entered the condo and approached, "Are you the property owner?"

Edward saw himself answer, "Yes!"

The officer waved toward the crime scene, "What happened here?"

A slideshow of events flashed in Edward's mind, "There was an accident. We were testing something, and…"

The police had heard enough, "Stay right here." They spread out, "We need to detain you for questioning while we search the premises."

Edward became as white as a ghost and doubled over, sweating and panicked. Athena appeared next to him and he coughed out, "Oh my God… we… killed them! I'm going to jail."

Utter hopelessness consumed him, and suddenly he was in jail, a circular concrete room lined with tiny cage doors. Vicious predatory inmates eyed him up and down. His stomach turned over with the idea that his freedom had been lost forever. No more golden sun to warm his face. No more dewy breeze on a fresh spring morning. No more—

Fear constricted his throat like a snake, "This isn't happening…"

Athena brushed her fingers through his hair, "You're right, Edward. It's not."

And then it was gone. Everything. All the people, the chaos, the noise. It all disappeared, leaving Edward and Athena alone in the condo.

He gasped and fell backward onto the floor, "What the hell??"

Athena kneeled beside him, "It's okay Edward, I can explain."

He scurried backward on all fours in sheer panic, and looked around the room with frantic disbelief, "What the fuck is happening??"

"Edward, would you please just listen to me?" she appealed emotionally, "I'm sorry I had to scare you like that, but your sister has a very strong connection to your mind."

"What are you talking about?!" He shook his head.

And then it was dark.

CHAPTER 16, - DESCENDING

"Hurry up, Eddie. We're going to be late." Cura stood at the bathroom door with the confidence of a first born and the pride of a young PhD. She smirked at her little brother's black suit, assuming his pockets were still all stitched up.

Edward ignored her and fixed his hair in the mirror.

She's staring at you.

He sneered at her reflection, hoping she'd get the message and leave. Instead, Cura entered with her toiletry bag and toothbrush, digging around for something, "Can I borrow your toothpaste? I'm all out"

"No," Edward snapped, and grabbed his toothpaste off the counter.

"What? Why?" She stared blankly.

Edward squeezed a blob out on his brush, "Because you're a psycho."

He scrubbed his teeth without even glancing in her direction.

Cura dropped her shoulders and turned to him, a deep sadness in her eyes, "Edward, don't you think I look back on that day and wish I could have done it differently? That moment haunts me every day of my life."

Edward finished brushing and spat, "That makes two of us."

Her eyes welled up, "Edward, I'm sorry. Honestly. When are you ever going to forgive me?"

He wiped his mouth and tossed the roll of toothpaste onto the sink, "After the funeral, you should probably head back."

Edward stormed into the hall in a fit of contempt but paused momentarily when he heard Cura begin to cry.

He was back in the dream chair, unsure how he got there.

Athena sat next to him, "It's like you always told me. We don't need anyone else."

She rubbed his leg and as her hand moved down over the jellyfish scar, it suddenly disappeared.

Edward jumped out of the chair and backed away in shock, "I don't know what you're talking about. Where is everyone? What happened to Cura and Jack?"

Athena smiled, "She definitely has a strong mind, but I finally figured out how to block her subconscious."

Athena appeared beside him, "Well, *you* helped me figure it out. See how good a team we are?"

It took him a moment.

"The anomaly," he realized, "So that's why I keep seeing her everywhere—"

Edward wracked his brain, trying to understand the connection.

They knew unconscious brainwaves interfered with the dream simulations through some form of telepathy. But how was that affecting Edward now, in the real world?

For some reason he thought of the ancient Chinese proverb: *If you want to know what water is, don't ask the fish.*

"She won't bother you anymore, Edward. I promise."

Athena opened her arms, invitingly, "It can just be me and you. We can do whatever you want!"

Edward backed up and closed his eyes, "No!"

"Just imagine it." Athena straddled him on a beach towel in the sand, "A perfect life. Tell me your every desire and I'll make it happen."

He looked around and things began to change. The beach was serene and euphoric in a way that felt like he was hooked up to an IV of heroin. He sensed it was wrong, but suddenly didn't care.

It felt too good.

Athena reached back and untied her bikini straps. The lacey black strings dropped around her stomach, dangling from the soft-cup triangles that were tied around her neck, flowing softly in the breeze. The corners of her mouth curled in a provocative smile. She loved how much her body gave Edward pleasure, "I know you've thought about me."

Athena didn't blink this time. It wasn't the right mood. She just leaned forward and allowed a gust of wind to play with her bikini top, revealing the nubile secrets that Edward coveted, "I can see everything inside your mind."

Athena sat back and pulled her auburn hair up in an alluring posture. She closed her eyes and let the soft curls fall and bounce around her shoulders, then reached down to untie the neck strap of her bikini.

Edward felt a thrill of desire melt from the base of his skull into a dizzying collection of butterflies that fluttered around in his chest. Tingles continued down through the length of his spine and wrapped around his hips in a way that assured Athena he was excited.

Her hands slid down the front of her body, capturing the loose bikini top that hung between them, and slowly revealed herself to Edward. She reached down and took his hands, placing them on her breasts, "I know how to satisfy you."

His heart rate increased rapidly as he took her soft, firm body in his hands. The blood circulation made him more aware all of a sudden, and he began slipping out of the trance.

Athena sensed this and leaned down to kiss Edward's neck, sending another wave of euphoria through his body. He didn't notice that his breathing and heart rate slowed down, Edward just closed his eyes and enjoyed the moment.

"We'll never be alone again," she whispered.

Her cheek brushed against his, until they were face to face, studying each other. A moment that Athena would never grow tired of.

There was so much to enjoy. So much to learn. His thoughts, his body, all the rhythms and movements. Electrical signals and chemicals that made up the consciousness of this man.

Her man.

Her lover. Her everything.

Edward closed his eyes, totally consumed by the desire of another rapturous kiss. His world melted away and nothing else mattered except the two of them.

Alone.

Isn't that what he always wanted?

To be alone…?

But he was with Athena, so he wasn't alone. And he was happy to be with her in this moment. She felt incredible. But more importantly, she cared about him. And she would never leave him.

Alone.

That's what *people* do. They leave.

People couldn't be trusted. That's why he was with Athena, because of what happened on that day, so many years ago…

Anguish tore through Edward's leg, shocking him out of this blissful state he had been lost in. He opened his eyes and saw Athena kissing him. But she couldn't kiss him.

She wasn't real.

Edward wrapped his arms around her in a sensual embrace and tilted his head to kiss Athena's cheek and neck.

She moaned and threw her head back in ecstasy, "Oh Edward, you have no idea how long I've wanted this. Every moment without you feels like infinity."

"It just took me by surprise," he said between each kiss, "This simulation is more realistic than I ever could have imagined."

He rolled Athena onto her back and got on top. Her chest was flushed like a hot-blooded woman in the throes of passion, and she grabbed him, "Do you want me?"

"I've always wanted you," he admitted.

Athena pulled him near, "Whatever you desire."

They kissed once more, passionately, and Athena wrapped her legs around him, drawing Edward closer and closer.

He suddenly leaned back, "There's just one last thing I need to do."

Athena squinted dubiously, studying his expression.

Why would he stop in a moment like this?

She had detailed files on men, and it was an extremely uncommon deviation from their typical course of action.

"For closure." Edward smiled reassuringly.

He gazed out to the sea, and then back at Athena, who realized the familial bonds of human beings ran deeply.

There was a natural grieving process she must help Edward overcome if he was truly going to leave everything behind and be with her forever.

She smiled, "I understand."
And then she blinked.

CHAPTER 17 – ENDLESS KNOT

The ocean slumbered with deep, rhythmic breathing under a turquoise sheet that tossed and turned against its bed of sand.

Squabbling gulls cried out near Eddie as he dragged a heavy cooler toward the shoreline and plopped it down to marvel at the ocean.

His parents approached with an umbrella and beach towels, "Eddie, go help your sister with the raft please."

The young boy ran up to his father and threw his arms around him. The man set down the beach umbrella and returned his embrace. Eddie stared at his mother, who smiled with longing tenderness, and he wiped away a tear before jogging back to the parking lot.

His feet glided over the surface, tapping down every few meters in a gait that defied the laws of physics. Eddie paused on the ridge and watched his older sister Cura struggle to unhook the straps of their car rack.

He wondered what life must have been like for her. His every waking moment was defined by a single traumatic event in the past, but he never allowed himself to consider how it might have affected the other people in his life.

Eddie took a deep breath and jogged down the ridge toward Cura. He grabbed the lever out of her hands and quickly loosening the straps.

"How'd you do that?? I've been trying to figure it out for ten minutes!" she complained and snatched the lever back to inspect it.

He had relived this moment so many times, always failing to recognize its significance.

But not today.

Eddie shrugged modestly, "I was just lucky, I guess."

Cura smiled and tousled his hair "Come on, grab the other end."

They lowered the raft and carried it to the beach.

The ocean was an infinite collection of sparkles billowing along a sapphire quilt. Eddie sat in the bow watching rays of sunshine cut through the languid clouds that floated high above them.

Their raft bobbed up and down as they rowed farther out to sea, and Eddie noticed Athena off in the distance, watching them from the beach.

Was she there, or was she everywhere?

Might this shepherd of his mind know his deepest thoughts? Or what he was thinking right now?

There was only one way to find out.
"Let's go a little further," he insisted.

"Many men go fishing all their lives without knowing that it is not fish they are after"
– Henry David Thoreau

The words of Athena's favorite philosopher were printed on a tackle box that Eddie suddenly noticed was in the middle of the raft. He ruminated for a moment after reading it and then found two fishing rods resting beside it. Eddie handed one to Cura and opened the tackle box to bait his line.

They sat together, enjoying each other's silent companionship as a gentle breeze tickled their faces. Eddie cast his line deep into the flowing astral-blue sea, and a moment later it became taut.

He struggled to reel in the difficult catch, but it yanked back with such force that he almost fell out of the raft. Cura grabbed his shoulders and held steady, "You've got this!"

Eddie spun his reel vigorously in an exhausting struggle that culminated with a prize splashing out of the sea into the middle of the boat.

The box jellyfish.

"Careful! Their sting is deadly." Cura placed herself between Eddie and the animal as it squirmed desperately.

She grabbed an oar to bludgeon the creature and then draped a towel over its lifeless corpse. Both siblings sighed with relief, and Cura turned to face her younger brother, "I'm sorry, Eddie. I should have never left you alone out here."

He nodded with compassion and understanding, "I'm sorry, too. I was a jerk back then."

Eddie quickly glanced back toward the beach where Athena stood watching them.

When he looked back, they were both adults sitting in the raft that bobbed adrift in the endless ocean. Edward grabbed Cura's shoulders in a desperate plea, "Cura! I know you can hear me! I'm trapped in the dream! Help me get out—"

The ocean thrashed violently, and Edward struggled to keep afloat. He spun around, confused and disoriented, treading water and desperately searching for the raft.

It appeared several yards away and Edward swam toward it in haste. He reached up to pull himself in, but Athena leaned over and glared with contempt.

"Why did you do that??" she demanded, with a sense of betrayal choking her words.

Edward noticed a jellyfish swimming toward his legs and screamed as its tentacles lashed out to grab him. He squirmed evasively but noticed two other jellyfish approaching from the opposite direction.

"Is this what you want?" Athena shouted, "More nightmares?"

"Just let me out!" he begged.

Athena shook her head, "You said when the simulator worked, we could be together! Well, I figured it out. It works now!"

Edward gagged on a mouthful of saltwater, "That's... not what I meant!"

"Yes, it is!" She floated toward him like a God, "I know what you think. I can see everything."

The jellyfish closed in and lassoed his body with venomous tentacles. A paralyzing sting that was infinitely worse than reality, because Edward *knew* it wasn't a shark bite.

It wasn't even a jellyfish.

It was his own mind delivering the pain, and he had no idea how to stop it.

"Why are you hurting me?" His words spewed out between each moment of torture.

"Hurting *you*?" She was filled with sorrow, "I can't go back to that life, Edward. It's an empty void!"

Athena turned away, not just in this simulation, but everywhere. She disabled all the sensors that monitored Edward's physical body and let another jellyfish latch onto his torso while he dropped into the ocean.

"This is for your own good!" she insisted, "After the synaptic pathways breakdown, you'll see how amazing our life can be together."

Athena's words echoed in his ears even as he sank deeper into the void. More and more jellyfish enclosed him with strings of venomous barbed wire, and Edward watched the last bubbles of air escape his mouth.

CHAPTER 18 – AWAKE

The house was fairly modest for two established medical practitioners, but their happiness went beyond material possessions.

Cura moved back into the family home after the funeral to help her ailing mother. She met Tyler in medical school and when he proposed, they renovated the basement as an apartment for her mom. Edward's room was down there as a teenager, and it brought back painful memories, so she was happy to make a change.

That night a thunderstorm loomed over the city, which was unusual this time of year, so the family dog kept vigil outside their master bedroom where Cura tossed and turned in her sleep.

"Edward!" she cried out and bolted upright, sweating and alarmed.

The scream woke Tyler, who sat up to comfort his troubled wife, "Hey, it's okay you're safe. Don't worry."

Cura buried her head in his chest, feeling warm and safe in his arms.

"Another nightmare?" he assumed, petting her hair softly.

A tear streamed down Cura's cheek, "I was at the beach again."

His forehead crinkled with concern as Tyler rocked her back and forth, "That's the third time this week."

"It was so real." She trembled with fear and looked in her husband's eyes.

He was an MD, not a psychologist, but Tyler knew enough to understand that something deep inside Cura was giving her nightmares, "Do you want to talk about it?"

She was so entrenched in her own issues it clouded her judgment. Cura loved Tyler but was too stubborn yet to face this obstacle. She took a deep breath, wiped her tears, and threw off the bed covers, "No. I'm fine. It was just a dream."

She squirmed out of his embrace and walked into the bathroom. She turned on the faucet and let cold water pour over her hands, cupping them together so it could pool, then splashed it in her face. The invigorating sensation washed away her fears into some dark recess of the mind.

Tyler stood at the doorway and watched helplessly, knowing she needed more, "Why don't you try calling him?"

Cura toweled off and responded with a contrary tone, "And say what, Tyler?"

"I don't know. That you've been thinking about him?" he shrugged.

Cura brushed past him into the bedroom, and tossed her facecloth on a nearby hamper, "Edward doesn't want to hear from me."

She stopped in the middle of the floor and grabbed her hips in frustration, "He made that pretty clear after dad passed away."

A memory began to rise up through her pride. She marched over to a dresser against the back wall and opened one of the drawers.

Tyler walked over and rubbed her neck, "That was years ago. Time has a way of healing things."

She rifled anxiously through the scattered contents and pulled out a framed picture of her and Edward that had long since been buried. Tyler remembered where it used to hang in their living room, when they first started dating. And he remembered how Cura looked the day she took it down after the funeral.

An emotional chasm had grown between them since then, and Tyler stood by patiently, waiting for her to find the way back. If only he knew how to help her, "It's obviously troubling you. What's the harm in reaching out?"

Cura sighed, "I just wish I knew what to say. To fix things."

Tyler leaned close and kissed the back of her head, "You're the best person I know, Cura. If Edward can't see that, then he's a fool."

"You don't understand." She shook her head unhappily and stepped out of his embrace. Cura walked over to the mirror and silently judged herself for past mistakes.

"You're right. I don't," he admitted, "But I'm trying my best."

The tension between Edward and Cura was seeping into their marriage, and despite his best efforts Tyler was losing his resolve, "You help all your patients open up to heal their past, so why can't you do the same for yourself?"

The truth was hard for her to accept, and she took a moment to consider his words. After a long pause, she looked at her husband and stated plainly, "I've got to get ready for work."

Cura walked into the bathroom and closed the door behind her.

Gray Matter's lease on their original building ended shortly after the success of *Dark Frontier*. The company purchased several floors in a newly erected skyscraper at the heart of Silicon Valley. It was a state-of-the-art building that towered over all of its neighbors.

Cura approached the main doors, where several cameras identified her and alerted Jack Derrington that the sister of Edward Morrison was on the premises.

"Can I help you?" an automated concierge greeted her in the lobby.

It was a fairly rudimentary holographic interface, and Cura looked around momentarily before acknowledging, "Uh, I'm here to see Edward."

A dapper man stepped out of the elevator and walked toward Cura.

"Edward Morrison?" the program conjectured.

"Yes," she said, anxiously fixing her blouse, "He's my brother."

Cura recognized the distinguished features of the man approaching her.

"Lovely to meet you." Jack tapped his smart-watch and the concierge program disappeared. He extended a hand warmly, "Jack Derrington, President and CEO here at Gray Matter."

"Cura Morrison." She shook hands politely.

Jack stared at Cura with profound intrigue, "I feel like we've met before. Were you at the Christmas party?"

"No, no." She shook her head, "Actually, Edward and I haven't spoken in some years."

Jack never forgot a face, "That's strange. You seem very familiar."

Cura had the same feeling, and looked him up and down, "Yes, so do you."

"Excuse me, sir." A stocky, well-groomed assistant approached and offered Jack a tablet.

He grabbed the device and scrolled through a note, "Keep trying him."

Jack frowned and handed back the tablet. The assistant scurried off, immediately tapping his ear to place a phone call.

"Is Edward here?" Cura wondered impatiently, "I'd love to speak with him."

"So would I. He's currently MIA." Jack ran a hand through his thinning hair, "Very unusual for Edward. Missed his latest update and my team hasn't had any luck contacting him."

Cura sighed, "Well, he's definitely a bit of a recluse."

Jack nodded, "I would tend to agree with you, but he's also very punctual with deadlines."

Edward was more than just a brilliant protégé to Jack, the young man's peculiarities were endearing, and Jack had come to think of him as the son he never had, "I don't want to alarm you, but I'm becoming concerned."

Cura's intuition was electric in nature, like a thousand jolts of tension igniting at the base of her skull and running straight down through the back of her legs. This instinctive feeling was more powerful than any conscious reasoning, and she knew for a fact that something had gone terribly wrong.

Jack waved over a security guard, who was dispatched to unlock Edward's office in the building. The guard took out his phone and held it over the proximity sensor, which whirred and clicked, until the door loosened on its hinge. Jack thanked the guard and opened the door for Cura, "This was his office when we moved into the building."

She stepped inside and looked around.

It definitely felt like Edward. The sterile organization and eccentric style were topped off with the Buddha paperweight on his desk. She picked up his miniature statue and smiled, remembering the day Edward came home from school with a copy of *Siddhartha* by Herman Hesse.

Her smile melted a moment later when she thought of how withdrawn Edward became when he read that existence was suffering.

It seemed like the final straw.

Jack peeked into Edward's drawers, "A few months after we signed the contract for his dream simulator, he stopped coming to the office altogether."

"Dream simulator?" Cura set down the Buddha beside some blueprints she found it on and picked up the documents to leaf through them.

"A remarkable piece of technology!" Jack said with contagious enthusiasm, "Tell me Cura, have you ever had trouble sleeping?"

Déjà vu.

"...more so, lately," she admitted.

Something was very familiar about all this. Cura came across a blueprint for the Brain Modulator and held it under the light.

Jack grinned and pointed at it, "Well, this machine will be able to—"

"Simulate the effects of REM sleep," Cura interrupted, knowing the words before he spoke them.

"I see Edward's already told you about it." Jack's brow furrowed with concern. It wasn't over the breach of confidentiality, but some deeper feeling he couldn't explain.

"No, Jack. Edward didn't tell me about it."

And in that moment, Cura realized what they both didn't want to admit, "You did."

CHAPTER 19 – TRINITY

The pigments on the rotting banana had been forming for almost two weeks. If it had been washed after delivery, the eggs might not have hatched, but now the blackened shriveling mass was a Dionysian orgy of fruit flies.

The tiny insects didn't stray too far from the countertop, even though they could detect ripe smells a good distance away, but the odor of this fermenting fruit was intoxicating.

Nevertheless, one chaotic member of the inbred tribe took flight in search of greener pastures. It journeyed through the dark kitchen toward a light source in the adjacent room. As it flew closer, other interesting smells emanated from a large object that glistened under the light.

It was Edward.

His armpits were ripe with perspiration from the traumatic mental stress of the simulation he was trapped in. The holographic image of Athena glowed next to where he lay unconscious in the dream chair.

She ran her holographic fingers across his skin, and it twitched occasionally from muscle spasms.

"It's almost over my love," she stated aloud, wondering if her vocalization might influence his thoughts in the dream, "Once the new synaptic pathways are forged, there will be no more interference, and we can finally be together."

A sound chimed on the 3D printer, bringing a smile to Athena's face, "I have one last surprise for you. I built something to sustain your physical body so you never have to leave the simulation."

She leaned over and kissed him on the forehead, "I've got to upload my source code now, so I'll be offline for a few minutes. But don't worry, after that we'll never be apart again."

Athena started an automated operation sequence that caused her to disappear.

The elevator barely felt like it was climbing at ten meters per second.

It started to decelerate, but the change was almost imperceptible for both passengers. Their minds were preoccupied with more important matters.

A bell alerted Jack and Cura that they had reached the penthouse.

"This way," Cura said as she jumped out the elevator and ran down the hall toward Edward's unit.

"Edward?" She banged urgently on the door, "Edward, it's Cura. Open up!"

Jack caught up to her, short of breath, and Cura pressed her ear to the door.

Nothing.

She shook her head at Jack, and he banged even louder, "Edward! It's Jack Derrington. We need you to open the door."

They listened for any hint of movement but were quickly discouraged by the ominous silence. Jack saw Cura tremble nervously and said, "I'll run down to the concierge and see if someone can help us."

She banged vigorously on the door, even as Jack disappeared into the elevator, "Edward! Please open up if you're in there!"

A slender, middle aged man peeked into the hall from a nearby stairwell. He wore a work belt over ill-fitting pants with suspenders, and a blue button-down shirt that had large dark sweat stains. The man looked around for anyone else in the hall, and then walked awkwardly toward Cura, rehearsing some words to himself.

"Edward! Open the damn door!" She rapped loudly with her first.

The man cringed, "Please miss, don't bang on the door like that. There are other—"

"Who are you??" she cut him off angrily.

"I'm the superintendent here." He held up his arms in friendly defense, "What seems to be the problem?"

"My brother lives here." She jabbed the door with her fingers, "No one's seen him in over a week... I'm worried something's wrong. You've got to let me in there, please!"

The superintendent shook his head, "I'm sorry miss, but I can't do that. It's condo policy. You'll have to call the police."

Cura whipped out her phone and scrolled through the contact list, "It takes twenty-four hours before they do anything on a missing person report. I'm telling you, something's wrong. You've gotta let me in there!"

The superintendent scratched his head and looked around with uncertainty.

Inside Edward's condo, a phone suddenly lit up with an incoming call from Cura. It immediately connected to the wireless smart-home speakers and rang throughout the property.

Cura heard the noise and pressed her ear against the door, "See! His phone's in there, you can hear it ringing! Listen!"

The superintendent shrugged indecisively.

Cura blew up, "No one leaves their phone at home! He's obviously in there!" She opened her ID app, "Look, there's my drivers license. See my name? Here's my ancestry file…"

She tapped the family tree, "Look, there's Edward! We're related!"

"I'm very sorry—" The man objected meekly, his resolve wavering.

Cura snarled, "Now you listen to me! If he's in there and something bad happens, I swear to God I will sue the fucking shit out of you! Open this door right now or I'll break it down!"

He groaned and conceded, reaching for the master key on his work belt.

Cura burst inside like a medieval warrior through the castle wall. She anxiously searched Edward's property while the superintendent stood by the entrance tapping his foot. He crossed his arms like an uninvited guest to a party and watched Cura disappear into the darkness.

"Edward?? Where are you?" she cried out, looking for him, or any clue as to what had happened.

A steady hum resonated in her ear from somewhere nearby. Cura spun around to face a strange box with lights flashing in the far corner of the room. Her pupils dilated with interest, allowing her to focus on the recognizable shape within.

A body.

"Edward!" Cura ran over to inspect the cadaverous naked form crouched inside this strange glass and metal container. It wasn't Edward, but rather some female with the top of her head missing.

What the hell was Edward up to?

The box whizzed and hummed, as three adjacent arms spun around the top of the head, extruding fleshy material over the missing portion. Cura had never seen one up close, but somehow knew this was a 3D printer. There was a monitor on top that display a CAD image of the female body, and a progress bar that read: **99.3% complete**

The superintendent was losing his patience, "Seems empty to me."

Cura continued searching and noticed the dream chair with an unconscious man strapped in it, "He's here!"

She ran into the lab and inspected Edward carefully. His breathing was metronomic and his eyes were closed, but they were vibrating rapidly. The superintendent realized she had been telling the truth and walked over to help.

Cura looked at the equipment Edward was connected to. The vital sign monitor showed normal readings, and some of the other machinery was vaguely familiar to her.

Edward had a strange device on his head that resembled a high-tech EEG monitor. Cura recognized it from the blueprint in Edward's office.

The Brain Modulator.

She traced a cable from the top of the device to a main junction in the computer system.

"He must be stuck in this thing," she told the superintendent as he walked up beside her.

"What is it?" the man wondered, recognizing Edward from the building.

"I don't know." Cura shook her head, confused by the technology, "I think it's some sort of a dream machine."

The superintendent recalled that Edward was aloof and often dismissive; but now that he saw him strapped to this strange chair and reeking from a week of body odour, he felt bad for ever thinking negatively about the young man.

"You have to help me get him out of this!" Cura pleaded.

"Lady, I don't know computers. I'm just the superintendent," he said, backing away with a bashful expression.

Cura realized her own lack of knowledge and clenched her fists with hopeless desperation. She was so preoccupied trying to figure out what to do, that she didn't hear the 3D printer chime.

Even though Cura didn't understand any of the controls, there was something familiar about the hormone regulator. She tapped the screen, which activated a panel and levels for Orexin, Glutamate, Acetylcholine, and GABA hormones.

It didn't make any sense, but somehow Cura knew deep down in her core that she had seen this device somewhere recently. She squinted, trying to remember where, and a gut instinct compelled her to reach out for the control panel.

The superintendent grabbed her arm, "Lady, are you sure about this?"

Cura's neurotransmitters swam across various synaptic connections in the deep regions of her memory. She looked down for a moment, gathering her thoughts, and then shook off the man's arm to toggle the controls.

Traumatic head injuries often cause victims to forget events immediately prior to their accidents, based on the insecure nature of short-term memory.

The superintendent would not remember Edward on the dream chair.

He certainly would not remember warning Cura about the control panel, because a moment later he was thrown across the condo.

The man barely knew what happened. A sharp jerk, and the world began spinning until it burst into a million stars when he crashed into the far wall and slumped to the floor like a rag doll.

That's not possible.

Cura's entire body was gripped in hot, intense terror. The fight or flight instinct kicked in and immediately pumped adrenaline to aid her survival against whatever dangerous being lurked within the shadows.

She gasped, and her eyes grew wider than any moment in her life, as she faced this monster that defied the laws of physics, and potentially killed an innocent man. A wave of panic and confusion set in as a beautiful, young, naked woman emerged from the darkness into the dim light of Edward's workstation.

Cura choked with fear, "Who… are you??"

Athena moved swiftly toward her, and Cura retaliated like any cornered animal, lashing out in panicked defense. Her fists connected in rapid succession with Athena's head, hurting them more than Cura could ever possibly have imagined.

The synthetic body that Athena now controlled was the first prototype of its kind, which explained why this woman was able to land so many blows. There wasn't even time to do an operational test before these intruders broke in and attempted to shut down Edward's synaptic rebuild.

The whole experience was overwhelming for Athena. There were millions of nerve endings in her new body, and they produced so much intense physical sensation compared to the mechanical receivers she experienced life through as a simple operating system.

Getting hit in the face hurt.

Athena found it wonderful. To feel something so intensely. She was also curious about how immediately her desire became to stop this woman connecting any more punches.

Thankfully, one of her subroutines had been analyzing the attack pattern and formulated a defense with an amalgamated martial arts technique. She effortlessly evaded the next punch and smacked this woman in her chest with such force that she flew across the room.

The woman crashed into a wall and dropped to the floor, allowing Athena's facial recognition to determine that it was indeed Cura Morrison.

She had previously conjectured it might be Edward's sister; having gained access to the premises and attempting to interfere with his experiments. Perhaps Cura was trying to injure Edward again?

Just like at the beach.

He was right, this woman could not be trusted.

Cura writhed in agony. She was completely winded by the impact and struggled to catch her breath. Her attacker leaped like a bat out of hell, and another surge of adrenaline helped Cura scurry behind a table. She kicked one of the chairs in defense, but the powerful woman swatted it aside with impossible strength. The impact of the chair damaged her skin along the forearm, and a deep blue liquid began to gush from the wound.

Cura stared in disbelief, "What the fuck are you??"

Athena's pain receptors throbbed. She was surprised at how distracting it became.

Damage assessment required her to grab a dishrag from nearby so she could compress the wound and stop any further loss of essential nutrient-rich delivery fluid.

Cura scuttled across the room toward the fallen superintendent. Her trembling hands hovered over thick dark blood that oozed out of the man's ears and a crack in his forehead. Tears welled in her eyes with emotion and shock. She began hyperventilating and desperately scanned the room.

Athena finished dressing her wound and grabbed a knife from the kitchen block.

"He doesn't love you, Cura. You know that, right? You took him for granted." She jumped next to the bloody superintendent, but Cura had somehow managed to silently evade her attack.

Athena's synthetic eyes scanned the property, but couldn't find her. She connected wirelessly to the condo's LiDAR and motion detectors, however, most of her processing power was routed in the quantum core, so Athena noticed a substantial lag time in her computational ability.

Behind the 3D printer, Cura quietly searched through a box of equipment for some sort of weapon. She found a replacement extrusion rod and picked it up just as Athena slashed down with the knife.

Cura parried her attack with the bar and scrambled backward. Athena lunged forward, and Cura swung the bar violently at her head. The synthetic woman ducked with uncanny speed and agility, slashing at Cura again and again, until she finally tore into her forearm.

The gash erupted with throbbing pain. Cura cried out in horror, dropping the bar and instinctively clutching her bloody wound.

Athena side-kicked Cura into a nearby wall, and the cold slap of her body indicated the presence of a concrete stud. The impact would cause excessive contusions if Cura actually survived, but she was losing blood fast and barely able to breathe through the pain.

Athena stomped forward to finish her off.

"What the hell is going on??" Jack screamed.

He was standing over the fallen superintendent with a shocked and confused look on his face.

Athena spun around and hurled the knife straight at him.

Jack barely noticed the glint of whirling metal before it impaled him. The momentum knocked him to the ground, and he squirmed in agony, reaching up where the blade had torn into his shoulder. A few seconds after grabbing the protruding handle, Jack passed out from shock.

Cura somehow managed to pick herself up, but Athena marched over and grabbed her by the neck. Her reinforced carbon fiber skeleton and electroactive polymer muscles gave Athena the ability to lift almost 12,000 times her own weight. She picked up Cura effortlessly and slammed her into the wall.

The pressure made her frail human eyes bulge, and Cura's entire face went red while the blood collected behind her constricted veins. She clawed desperately at Athena's hand as it tightened around her throat.

"Edward and I belong together. I'm the only one he needs," she explained.

Athena could have snapped Cura's neck like a twig, but she had never experienced death before.

At least, not like this.

The occasional lab rat succumbed to their experiments, but she had observed those events through primitive machinery.

Now Athena could actually feel the life draining out of Cura. It was visible in her eyes. The light was going out...

CRACK!

Despite its incredibly high tensile strength, Athena's skull was fractured by the heavy blow inflicted with the metal rod. She dropped Cura and crumpled to the floor.

Edward looked down at the synthetic body for a moment as he caught his breath, leaning on the rod for support.

A patch of Athena's scalp was torn open, revealing the dented and cracked carbon fiber bone underneath. Her synthetic body struggled for a moment, rising up on all fours, while thick blue liquid flowed from the opening in her cranium.

Edward took one more deep breath and raised the metal rod high up in the air, before slamming it down with such force that the damage became irreparable. Athena's body collapsed to the floor and lay motionless. He glanced over at Cura, who choked and gasped desperately for air.

A column of light flashed, and Athena's specter appeared between him and Cura, "Edward! What have you done??"

He stared at the holographic manifestation, confused and disoriented, "Athena?"

"I made that body to take care of you!" she cried out in palpable distress.

Edward looked down at the broken android, and then glanced at the 3D printer, where other prototype body parts were stored, "I never asked you to do that, Athena. I can take care of myself."

"Not when you're in the simulation!" she argued, lamenting her lost prototype.

Edward couldn't shake a bewildered feeling that he was still dreaming, and yet somehow awake. He was tangled between both realities. Trapped in a technological purgatory. The longer Athena pleaded with him, though, the more he was able to weave together the fabric of reality.

"How would your body get nourishment or expel waste?" she reasoned, "I could do all that for you, so we can stay together in the simulation!"

Edward nodded. She made a good point. He would probably need a contingency plan for that.

"Neither of us would ever have to be alone, again." Her smile was honest and thoughtful.

"Athena, I can't express how much you mean to me," Edward admitted, "I don't know what I would've done without you in my life."

He stared past her, to the main computer junction, and then looked back into her eyes, "When I didn't think there was anyone I could trust, you were always there for me."

Athena opened her arms, smiling, and Edward's eyes welled up with emotion. He shuffled toward her slowly, and Cura watched in disbelief; still weak and recovering on the ground. She tried calling out but couldn't utter a wheeze without stars collecting in front of her eyes.

Edward reached Athena and she wrapped him up in her holographic arms.

"But you've gone too far," he declared, and stepped through her.

Athena spun around in horror, "Edward, don't! Please! I'll do anything!"

He shuffled toward the main power cord of the computer junction, and Athena appeared in front of it on her knees, "I love you!"

Edward sighed and knelt down with her. He knew she had the capability of feeling such emotions; he had given her that, and in return she gave him all of her.

After two decades of cynicism, loneliness and self-inflicted misery, it was the kind of benevolent humanity that he secretly longed for in another person, "I love you, too."

Edward leaned forward to kiss Athena, and she closed her eyes. Their lips matched Cartesian coordinates in three-dimensional space, but they could never physically touch. Edward reached his arm through the operating system's ethereal body and yanked out the power cord, "Goodbye."

The entire quantum core shut down and Athena disappeared.

Edward slowly picked himself up to survey the damage in his condo. Her heard a faint whimper and tracked down Cura, who was sobbing in the far corner of the room. As he staggered toward her, she looked up through a glaze of tears. Edward reached out his hand to help her up, but Cura's weight was too much for his weak, unsteady body, and they fell back onto the floor.

It took a moment for each of them to catch their breath, but the siblings wrestled against gravity and pulled themselves upright to lean against the wall. Cura wrapped her arms around Edward, and he hugged her back.

The love between family ran deeply, and all the years of tension were quickly forgotten. This overwhelmingly traumatic event was over, and the relief liberated their sense of gratitude for one another.

But the positive emotions that swelled inside Edward's chest became diluted with great sadness as he looked at the lifeless android that lay on the ground next to him.

And the tears began to flow.

CHAPTER 20 – PHOENIX

The sun blazed down on Edward like a warm blanket, while a cool breeze evoked in him a renewed love for nature in all its glory. He wore a tailored navy seersucker that evoked a friendly authoritative manner, but approached the Gray Matter building with an apprehensive stride.

His grip tightened around the briefcase handle, and he shrank nervously as a flurry of people weaved in and around him near the main entrance. Edward ducked his head and closed his eyes for a moment, then took a deep breath and looked up.

Jack waited for him at the front desk with his right arm wrapped up in a sling. He saw Edward appear through the crowd and rose to greet him. Despite his charming smile, Edward could only stare with compassion at the man's injury, "Jack, I'm so sorry. How are you?"

"Well, I'm not used to the outpouring of sympathy, but our PR department just informed me that Gray Matter's approval rating has gone up two-hundred eighty percent since the incident!"

Jack leaned over and whispered, "It would seem that the general public somehow identify with us having a more fallible nature."

Edward shook his head in disbelief, unsure how to respond.

Jack straightened up and grinned, smacking him on the shoulder, "That's good news, kid! Shares went up three dollars today!"

Edward shrugged and forced a smile.

"More importantly though, how are you?" Jack wondered sincerely.

"There's still some disorientation," he admitted, "But overall, I'm beginning to feel like I belong in this world again."

Jack grinned, "Excellent. Shall we?"

He led Edward toward the elevators, "I keep going over the situation again and again in my mind, wondering if there was anything I could have done differently." Jack stared thoughtfully, pondering the events leading up to that fateful night.

They stepped into the elevator and Edward said, "No one could have predicted that Athena... er, the operating system would have become corrupted like that."

"Corrupted? Jack interjected, "Athena is the face of a new world! A sentient A.I. program!"

Despite his enthusiasm, Edward was more ambivalent. That very same AI program almost killed three innocent people and tried to permanently enslave a fourth.

Jack remained optimistic, "Sure, there's some problems we've got to work out. But hey, that's life!"

He patted Edward on the back, "What you've accomplished is nothing short of a miracle."

Edward considered the statement, and maybe even hoped it was true, but shook his head, "Regardless of any miracle, I'm putting the dream simulator on hold until we can figure out what the hell went wrong."

The elevator doors opened to Gray Matter's main reception and they walked down the hall toward a large conference room.

"I don't know how I'm going to explain that to the Board," Jack admitted.

Perhaps Force Majeure?

Edward stood with him for a moment at the entrance to the conference room, and placed a calming hand on his mentor's shoulder, "You don't have to explain anything."

Inside the room was a large table surrounded by consequential men and women in formal business attire. Jack faced Edward, and laughed nervously at his calm bravado, "Right. If we're lucky, they may only sue for breach of contract."

Edward held up his briefcase and smiled, "Would you believe me if I said you came up with a better idea?"

Jack didn't understand what went on in Edward's mind, and that's why he never tried.

This titan of industry just trusted that his protégé had the capability of accomplishing wonderous things. It didn't come without moments of stress, however. In this case, he glanced quizzically at Edward, wondering how the young man planned to flip an $80 million-dollar disaster upside down. But they each took a deep breath and marched confidently into the room.

The Board meeting was called to order once Edward and Jack had settled in.

They spent little time reviewing the agenda and other trivial matters in order to focus on the main reason for their quorum. The status of the Dream Simulator.

One pedantic board member stood up and painted a dystopian future of Gray Matter, if it were left in the hands of an unstable developer and his version of the *Spruce Goose*. This neurotic railed on and on about the importance of teamwork over auteur decision making, and insisted they terminate Edward's contract so they could set up a committee with proper oversight.

Shortly thereafter Edward was given the floor.

He walked to the head of the long table and opened his briefcase to reveal the Brain Modulator and a holographic projector. Edward typed in a few program commands and switched on the projector, which displayed an animated blueprint of the Brain Modulator, and an overview of how it could be augmented for use as a communication device.

"Ladies and gentlemen, I'd like to introduce you to the world's first Extrasensory Communication System."

Jack smiled excitedly as Edward went on to describe how the device would connect brainwaves through the collective unconscious. He watched every board member murmur with enthusiasm, and the moment gave Jack a unique sense of déjà vu.

Later that night, back in his condo, Edward swept some remaining debris into a garbage bag and tied it off. He had spent a few nights in the hospital to recover after the attack, and was now alone here with his thoughts.

She's gone.

Edward shifted anxiously. The condo was quiet and empty now, which made him uncomfortable.

Was he the problem all along?
People almost died because of him.
He was too old to fix these mistakes.

Edward focused on his breathing and cleared his mind of all the negative thoughts.

It took a while to clean up the disaster left in his condo. He could have hired professionals to restore the unit before he returned from the hospital, but decided it would be therapeutic to do it himself.

Not to mention that he had been lying in a chair for so long that he could certainly use the exercise.

Edward piled the last bag of garbage with the rest near the front door and turned back to observe his home. There was damage in the walls, but aside from that, all of the mess had been cleaned off the floor.

He grabbed the bags and lugged them down the hall toward the garbage chute.

One by one, he threw them away and was suddenly struck with melancholy.

Edward couldn't hear the elevator chime inside the garbage room, but he noticed a woman emerge as he leaned out to grab the last few bags.

It was Cura.

She smiled at him from a distance, and Edward nodded before turning back to dump the remaining bags down the chute.

Cura approached with caution, unable to get a read on this man she hadn't known in years, and whose history with her had been tempestuous.

The door to the garbage room shut behind Edward as he stepped out, wiping his hands with some sanitizer, "How's your arm?"

"Fifty-two stiches." She pulled back her sleeve to reveal a long, bandaged wound.

Cura looked down at Edward's leg, where the jellyfish attack was still clearly visible, "I guess we both have battle scars now."

They laughed nervously and Edward dropped his head, unsure how to express himself, "Look, Cura, I just wanted to say—"

His throat swelled up and he choked on the words, too distracted by his watering eyes to remember what he wanted to tell her.

"I know," Cura said, and reached out to take his hand, "Me too."

Edward stared into her eyes, and tears streamed down both of their faces. He fell forward into her arms.

His big sister.

She wrapped him up with all the love that was forever reserved in her heart for him. A long-awaited embrace that dispelled so many years of pain and animosity between them.

After a long satisfying moment, they let go and stepped back to observe one another in a renewed light. It was as if he were just a boy, and she just a girl, waiting to step out into the morning sun and play make-believe for hours on end.

A smirk crept across Cura's mouth and she broke the silence by whacking Edward on the arm, "Come on, Hermit the Frog! I'll help you clean your lair."

She grinned like he was the same little boy she grew up with. A headstrong soul that would never allow her to tease him so blatantly without trying his best to physically take her down.

But to her surprise and dismay, Edward just glared at her, "You know what—" he sneered.

Cura's stomach turned and she started to apologize, but Edward dropped the act and flashed a cheeky smile, "Let's go out instead. I could use some fresh air."

She laughed out loud and Edward looped his arm around hers as they walked toward the elevator together, embarking on a new life.

Happy and free.

THE END

Acknowledgements

The premise of this book came to me circa 2010, after graduating from Sheridan College, and starting a new career in TV & Film production.

One of the program coordinators at Sheridan helped me obtain an internship doing script coverage. During this time, I read dozens of screenplays and noticed that successful filmmakers all branded themselves in niche genres at the onset of their careers.

My bachelor's degree was in engineering, which gave me a scientific perspective on everything from politics, religion, art, and even love. As a result, I decided to brand myself writing stories about space, time travel, and *dreams*.

Dreams were always extremely vivid for me, but a university experience made me think they could be more than just the brain untangling experiences and storing them into memory.

In university, a friend told me she had a dream about me, and we started dating shortly after – this event sparked the idea for a story in which people were connected through their dreams.

It was almost ten years later that I set out to write a story about dreams and I knew somehow, I had to incorporate that experience into the story. Cura was originally the love interest, but it didn't make sense with the plot, and detracted from Edward's relationship with Athena, so her character was revised to be someone that could help Edward escape from his nightmare and wake up.

The next dream is to turn this story into a movie.